Staffordshire Library and Information Services
Please return or renew by the last date shown

If not required by other readers, this item may may be renewed in person, by post or telephone, online or by email.
To renew, either the book or ticket are required

24 Hour Renewal Line
0845 33 00 740

Staffordshire
County Council

www.staffordshire.gov.uk

The Unknown

By the same author

Freedman
Soldier, Sail North
The Wheel of Fortune
Last in Convoy
The Mystery of the *Gregory Kotovsky*
Contact Mr Delgado
Across the Narrow Seas
Wild Justice
The Liberators
The Last Stronghold
Find the Diamonds
The Plague Makers
Whispering Death
Three Hundred Grand
Crusader's Cross
A Real Killing
Special Delivery
Ten Million Dollar Cinch
The Deadly Shore
The Murmansk Assignment
The Sinister Stars
Watching Brief
Weed
Away With Murder
A Fortune in the Sky
Search Warrant
The Marakano Formula
Cordley's Castle
The Haunted Sea
The Petronov Plan
Feast of the Scorpion
The Honeymoon Caper
A Walking Shadow
The No-Risk Operation
Final Run
Blind Date
Something of Value
Red Exit
The Courier Job
The Rashevski Icon
The Levantine Trade
The Spayde Conspiracy
Busman's Holiday
The Antwerp Appointment
Stride
The Seven Sleepers
Lethal Orders
The Kavulu Lion
A Fatal Errand
The Stalking-Horse
Flight to the Sea
A Car for Mr Bradley

Precious Cargo
The Saigon Merchant
Life-Preserver
Dead of Winter
Come Home, Toby Brown
Homecoming
The Syrian Client
Poisoned Chalice
Where the Money Is
A Dream of Madness
Paradise in the Sun
Dangerous Enchantment
The Junk Run
Legatee
Killer
Dishonour Among Thieves
Operation Zenith
Dead Men Rise Up Never
The Spoilers
With Menaces
Devil Under the Skin
The Animal Gang
Steel
The Emperor Stone
Fat Man From Colombia
Bavarian Sunset
The Telephone Murders
Lady from Argentina
The Poison Traders
Squeaky Clean
Avenger of Blood
A Wind on the Heath
One-Way Ticket
The Time of Your Life
Death of a Go-Between
Some Job
The Wild One
Skeleton Island
A Passage of Arms
On Desperate Seas
Old Pals Act
Crane
The Silent Voyage
The Angry Island
Obituary for Howard Gray
The Golden Reef
Bullion
Sea Fury
The Spanish Hawk
Ocean Prize
The Rodriguez Affair
Bavarian Sunset

The Unknown

James Pattinson

ROBERT HALE · LONDON

© James Pattinson 2008
First published in Great Britain 2008

ISBN 978-0-7090-8508-9

Robert Hale Limited
Clerkenwell House
Clerkenwell Green
London EC1R 0HT

www.halebooks.com

2 4 6 8 10 9 7 5 3

Printed and bound in Great Britain by
Biddles Limited, King's Lynn

CONTENTS

1

PROJECT

George Craydon had never been keen on the idea right from the start. He had been more or less dragged into taking part in the project by his wife. It might be all very fine, he said, for people who had notable characters back there in the family archives, but who ever heard of a Craydon doing anything worth writing home about?

'We're nonentities, that's what we are. Always in the rank and file. Menials, that's us.'

'I'm not a menial,' Joyce said. 'What's more, I wasn't even a Craydon until I married you. I was a Tate, remember?'

'Oh, I remember. But what has a Tate ever done? Tell me that. Apart from selling sugar, that is.'

'There's a Tate Gallery, isn't there? And there's probably a lot more stuff if we only knew. That's the kind of thing we might find out. And there'll be other names too, lots of them. The further back you go, the more you find. It's a tree, you see. It has loads of branches. It's going to be fun.'

George, forty-five years old, going bald and developing a paunch, worked in a bank and looked forward to the day when he would retire on a pension and no longer have to do a job that bored him. Joyce, two years younger and still not unattractive, helped part-time in a charity shop. They had a son and daughter who were both grown up and had flown the nest some time ago. They lived in a three-bedroom, semi-detached house in a quiet cul-de-sac in Ilford, with a little garden at the front and a rather larger one at the back. The mortgage had been paid off several years ago and they had no debts worth speaking of.

Taking one thing with another, George would sometimes reflect, they had little to grumble about. Not, of course, that this prevented a bit of grumbling at times.

'Everybody's doing it,' Joyce said.

'Even if that were true, which of course it isn't, it wouldn't be any good reason why we should.'

'Well, the Ropers are at it. Molly told me they'd found a great uncle who was a captain in the infantry in World War One.'

George sneered. 'A captain, eh? Big deal.'

'Well, it's something.'

The Ropers lived in the house next door, from which they were separated by no more than the thickness of a shared wall. Tom was a travelling salesman, but the Craydons had never been able to discover what it was that he sold. He was away from home for much of the time, but this did not appear to bother Molly. He was over fifty and she was fifteen years younger. They had no children and appeared to have no desire for any. George said this was just as well, because who would want parents like them? Joyce said he ought not to say things like that even if it was true. Which maybe it was. Though she quite liked Molly and could never understand why she had got herself hooked up to a pig like Tom.

She was quiet for a while. Then: 'I think we should go and see Aunt Maud.'

'What on earth for?'

'Well, she's donkey's years old and if anyone can give us some information about our ancestors she'd be the one.'

'Your ancestors,' George said. 'She's not my aunt.'

'Now don't be pernickety. We can do your lot later.'

'It wouldn't bother me if we didn't do them at all. Anyway, where's this Aunt Maud of yours living? If she is still living.'

'Of course she is. We'd have heard if she wasn't. She's got a cottage out in the backwoods.'

'What backwoods would they be?'

'Suffolk actually. A village called Long Seaton.'

'How do you know all this?'

'I write to her sometimes.'

George stared at her in disbelief. 'Are you telling me you actually write letters in this age of the internet and the e-mail?'

'She doesn't go in for things like that. She's over ninety, you know, and she's never caught up with modern technology.'

'And at that age I don't suppose she ever will. So you write to her, do you?'

'Well, when I say write I mean I send her a card at Christmas and on her birthday.'

'And does she respond?'

'My God!' Joyce said. 'Don't you notice anything? Of course she does.'

'And now you're proposing we should go and pick her brains. Is that it?'

'Why not? It'll be a nice outing. Perhaps the week after next. Or maybe the one after that, to give her time to reply to my letter.'

'Which you're proposing to write straightaway?'

'Yes.'

It was a fine September day when they started on the journey to the backwoods, and from the house in Ilford it was not much more than thirty miles.

'Maybe we should have called on the old girl before,' George said. 'She's probably lonely.'

'So now you're feeling guilty, are you?'

'Aren't you?'

'Maybe I am. A little. I've thought about suggesting it now and then but never got round to it.'

'Until you want to make use of her.'

'That's not a nice way of putting it. But yes, I suppose it is the truth.'

Molly Roper had been in her front garden when they set off. She came out on to the pavement and spoke to Joyce as she got into the car.

'We've found another one. Name of Bridges. Lived up north. Darlington. Had a bakery. Nineteenth century.'

'Good for you,' George said. 'A baker! That really is something.'

Joyce smacked him on the arm. 'Don't be snotty.' She turned to the other woman. 'Take no notice of him. He thinks it's all a waste of time. As a matter of fact we're off ancestor-hunting ourselves. An aged aunt may have memories.'

'If she isn't gaga,' George said.

'There's no reason to suppose she is. Not all old people are, you know. Some of them have sharper brains than others half their age.'

'Well, anyway,' Molly said, 'I wish you luck. And at least you've got a nice day for an outing even if you don't strike gold.'

They stopped at an inn for lunch. It turned out to be a remarkably good one and they did not hurry over it. They reached Long Seaton at around three o'clock in the afternoon. It was a rather larger village than they had expected.

It even had a post office and a couple of shops as well as two public houses and a church.

'I understood villages were dying,' George said. 'Everybody moving into towns. But it seems that some are hanging on to life.'

'And a good thing too. I've always had a feeling I'd like to live in a village.'

George scoffed. 'You wouldn't, you know. You'd be bored stiff. Nothing going on.'

'How do you know nothing goes on? Maybe there's quite a lot of social activity. Perhaps more than there is where we live.'

'You could be right at that.'

They stopped and asked a passer-by whether he could direct them to Willow Cottage.

The man, who was wearing a rather frayed cloth cap and a tweed jacket that came down almost to his knees, seemed happy to oblige.

'Willow Cottage. That'd be where Miss Waters lives.'

'That's right. Can you tell us how to get there?'

He could and he did, in great detail. They thanked him and headed for journey's end, which turned out to be some way down a narrow, potholed lane with unkempt hedges on each side.

Willow Cottage stood well back from the road, and there was a front garden that had a rather neglected appearance. The cottage itself was obviously old and the brickwork was very much weathered where it was not covered with ivy. The roof was thatched and the straw looked quite new, as though it had been renewed fairly recently. The tops of some willow trees were visible in the rear, and these had no doubt given the cottage its name; or were perhaps descendants of those that had.

George parked the Volkswagen on the overgrown grass verge and they sat for a few moments gazing at the cottage.

'Pretty little place,' he said. 'What you might call picturesque. Fetch quite a bit on the open market, I shouldn't wonder. The sort of place rich people buy for a weekend retreat. Far from the madding crowd and all that jazz.'

'Possibly. But it doesn't happen to be on the open market.'

'No. There'd be an estate agent's signboard sticking up if it was. Well, let's go and see the old dear.'

An iron gate squeeled for lack of oil on the hinges as they pushed it open, the bottom dragging on some weedy gravel of the path leading up to the front door.

There was a knocker shaped like a laurel wreath, but before they could use it the door was opened by a very old lady in a black dress.

'Ah!' she said, 'There you are, my dears. I've been keeping watch from the window and I saw you arrive. Do you know yours is the first car to come down here for at least half an hour. Not many people live on this lane and it leads nowhere, you see.'

She was not at all what George had expected. For no reason at all he had imagined a large, rather domineering woman with a loud voice. Aunt Maud was not a bit like that. She was diminutive and her voice was hardly above a whisper. Her face was round and wrinkled, like an apple that had remained on the shelf all winter, and she wore a pair of glasses with steel frames.

'Now do come inside. Joyce, you're a naughty girl. You should have come to see me ages ago.'

'I know. And I've always been meaning to. But you know how it is. Things get put off.'

Aunt Maud gave her hand a little pat. 'Of course. Young people have so much to occupy their time. But let's not stand here. Come into the sitting-room.'

Joyce noticed that she did not call it a lounge. If the house had been larger she would probably have referred to it as a drawing-room. It was small and much of the space was taken up by a sofa and two armchairs with loose covers. There was a fireplace with a screen in front of it and a mantelpiece above crowded with small ornaments and a clock in a glass dome with a revolving pendulum going first one way and then the other. A portable television set on a table in one corner seemed to be the only modern feature in the room.

'So,' Aunt Maud said when they were all seated, 'you've caught this craze for ancestor hunting.'

Which showed, Joyce reflected, that old as her aunt

might be she was not unaware of what was going on in the world. In fact she gave every indication of being a pretty spry old lady who might be a trifle deaf but had all her wits about her.

'George hasn't,' Joyce said. 'He's only here on sufferance. But I think it's fun. You never know what you might find until you start looking.'

'Could be some black sheep, my dear. Have you thought of that?'

'Oh, I hope there are. It would make it more exciting. Do you know of any?'

'Only Uncle Thomas. My uncle, that is. Died years ago. You haven't heard of him?'

'No. What did he do?'

'It seems he was treasurer of some charity. Ran off with the funds and lost it all on the roulette tables in Monte Carlo.'

'Oh dear! Did he go to prison?'

'No. Committed suicide. Threw himself in front of a train. I was a child at the time and I didn't hear about it until years later. I have a vague memory of him as a smartly-dressed man with black hair and a moustache and side whiskers.'

George was sitting up and taking notice now. 'Well, well! A skeleton in the cupboard.'

'Not your cupboard,' Joyce said.

'Of course not. The Craydons have always been an honest lot.'

'As far as you know.'

'Now, now,' Aunt Maud said. 'No bickering, please. I've got some photographs which I think might interest you.'

She went to a cupboard on one side of the fireplace, opened it and took a large cardboard box from a shelf inside. This she carried to a table by the window. Joyce stood up and joined her, but George remained sitting. Aunt Maud removed the lid of the box to reveal that it contained a jumble of photographs of varying sizes and no kind of order.

'I've always meant to put them in an album but never got round to it.'

She upended the box and the photographs fell in a heap on the table. Most were the usual kind of amateur snapshots, some with dates and names on the back but many with no identification mark at all. Fortunately Aunt Maud had a remarkably good memory and was able to name members of the family whom Joyce had never met; many having been dead long before she was born. There was even one of the miscreant Thomas in a stiff white collar and with his hair parted in the middle.

'He looks quite honest.' Joyce said.

Aunt Maud gave a shake of the head. 'You never can tell by their looks, my dear. Who would have thought Crippen was a murderer?'

'Who was Crippen?' George asked; suddenly showing interest.

'Before your time, young man. Before mine too as a

matter of fact. Poisoned his wife and ran off with a floozie named La Neve or some such. They caught him on a ship going to America. She was dressed as a boy.'

'Well, well! The things they got up to in those days.'

'Now here,' Aunt Maud said, 'are some that might really interest you.'

The photographs she had picked out were quite small, about two and a half inches by three, but they were professional jobs; very old but still in perfect condition. One of them had printed on the back. Edwin T. Watson, The Studio, Haymarket, Norwich. It had a number on it: 628. There was also the information that further copies could be had on application. Written on it very lightly in pencil one could read: Uncle William. Aged 75, 1870.

The picture was of a white-haired man sitting on a Victorian armchair, probably with horsehair upholstery. He had a small beard and was wearing a dark suit and a bow-tie. One hand was resting on a small table beside the chair and the other was on his knee.

'Even I don't remember him,' Aunt Maud said, 'but I believe he was a solicitor.'

'An honest one, let's hope,' George said.

'It would hardly make any difference now whether he was or not. But let's give him the benefit of the doubt.'

They continued sorting out the old photographs and came to one of a young girl, possibly sixteen or seventeen years old.

'Oh, she's pretty,' Joyce said.

George got up to take a look and he too was impressed. 'She certainly is. A real beauty. Who is she?'

Joyce turned the card over and read: Isabella. Age 16½ . There was no date. She was standing and looking straight at the camera with a faint smile which might have had a trace of mockery in it. Her hair hung down in ringlets on each side of her face and she was wearing a white frock, taken in at the waist. She had white stockings and black shoes with silver buckles. She had obviously been dressed for the occasion and was maybe making something of a joke of it.

'Ah!' Aunt Maud said. 'That's Bella. One of the Fosters.'

The way she said it made Joyce look up. 'You knew her?'

'Oh dear me no. She was gone before I was born.'

'Gone? You mean she was dead?'

'Almost certainly. But also gone away. There was some mystery about her, and as a child I was never told anything to do with her. In fact her name was hardly ever mentioned in my hearing. It was as if there was some dreadful secret regarding her that mustn't be mentioned in front of the children. Later I lost interest, so I really don't know what happened to her.'

'What a pity. Sounds as if it might be worth hearing. Obviously she didn't have any children or you'd have known about them.'

'Oh yes. It's rather a wonder really that this photograph should have survived.'

'Are there any others? When she was older perhaps.'

'None at all. At least not in my collection. I doubt whether any exist. You can keep that one if you like. In fact you may as well take the lot. I don't really want to keep them.'

'You're sure?'

'Quite sure. This is the first time I've looked at them for years, and if they're of any interest to you you're welcome to them.'

'Well, thank you very much. And if we discover any interesting items of family history we'll come and let you know.'

'Is that a promise?'

'Yes, it's a promise.'

'Well mind you keep it.'

She insisted on providing them with some refreshment before they left: tea and cakes. These were brought in by a plump middle-aged woman whom she introduced as Mrs Biggs. She was a home-help, and Aunt Maud admitted that she had no idea how she would have managed without this competent and good-natured woman.

'I should have had to go into an old people's home.' She gave a little shiver. 'Perish the thought.'

'That won't happen while I'm around,' Mrs Biggs said. 'You can be sure of that.'

On the way home George remarked that the old girl appeared to be quite contented.

'How's she situated financially?'

'She was a teacher. Finished as headmistress of a primary school, so she'll have a decent pension, index-linked. She may have quite a bit put away.'

'I hope she's made a will. With us in it.'

'Don't be so mercenary.'

'Well, better us than a cats' home.'

Joyce smacked his arm. But the thought had been in her mind too, even though she did not admit it.

After a while George said musingly: 'That Isabella; I wouldn't be surprised if she was the most interesting one of all your lot. She was a real charmer, judging by that photograph. I'd really like to know what happened to her. The others must have known something.'

'Well, whatever they may or may not have known, they were obviously not passing the information on to Aunt Maud, and she's the only one who comes anywhere close to being a contemporary. So if she knows nothing it's dead certain nobody else in the family will have a clue. I'm afraid we shall just have to write dear Bella off as an unsolved mystery.'

2

EXECUTION

She had told herself that she would not go to the execution, that nothing in the world could persuade her to be a witness to that gruesome event. It would be too horrifying. It would live with her for the rest of her life. It would haunt her. It would be in her dreams, her nightmares for ever. There was every reason she could think of for not going. Strong reasons. Indeed, the strongest.

And yet she had come.

It was not as though she were not involved, that she could attend simply as one of these hundreds of others who had come to enjoy the spectacle. Here they all were, gathered shoulder to shoulder on the ground or gazing from the windows of private houses and the hotels that must have been doing excellent business that day. No doubt rooms overlooking the square had been reserved for days, if not weeks, ahead. Many of those who were here had, she imagined, been early enough to observe the erection of that grim instrument which had been specifically designed for the efficient severing of a human head from the body to which until that moment it had been for a lifetime attached.

It was an instrument that had taken its name from Dr Guillotin, who had proposed its use as a more humane method of execution than the axe. It had acquired its evil reputation in the Reign of Terror when aristocrats and others were taken to it in tumbrels while the citizens looked on and cheered. Even Robespierre was forced to submit his neck to it in the end. Now, although the victims of Madame la Guillotine came to her only singly the crowds still gathered to watch an execution.

And she was there with them, unrecognised by all those pressing around her but the only one among those hundreds who had so intimate an interest in what was soon to happen.

By dint of much perseverance she had forced her way almost to the front of the crowd where she was so close to that dread instrument that she could see its every detail. A man, whom she took to be the executioner, had tested it by drawing the massive triangular blade to the top of the frame and then releasing it, as though to make quite sure that it would perform its duty satisfactorily when the time arrived.

As if there could really be any doubt of that!

It had made her shudder, anticipating in her mind the fearful moment when a human neck would be there to provide some slight resistance to the final inches of the blade's descent.

She was living that moment already, though she knew that it might not come for another hour or possibly more. She felt a weakness in her legs and wondered whether they would continue to support her throughout the ordeal. Suppose she were to collapse and be trampled underfoot by the crowd. She caught snatches of conversation, ribald comments, laughter even, and she resented it. To these oafs it was nothing but an entertainment, almost as if it had been arranged simply for their benefit.

To her it was all so different. She felt as though she herself were a participant in the performance, not a mere member of the audience. And in a way she was; for had she not been involved in much that had led to this final scene of the drama? Or, to be more precise, the tragedy.

As time passed she had a feeling that the crowd was becoming impatient. Many of them had been there since early morning. Some of the more provident had brought food and drink with them. Those in the hotels were no doubt being well supplied. Some she could see had spyglasses in order to get a better sight of the proceeding. Nobody wanted to miss a moment of performance.

Those with the best positions were the first to catch sight of the main players in the drama but the news quickly spread to the rest and a hush fell on the gathering.

It was the priest whom she saw first. He had a book in

his hand from which he appeared to be reading, although she could not hear his voice. He was walking backwards, facing the condemned man, as though to hide from his sight the dread instrument that must end his life.

Then she saw the man. It was the first time in weeks. She might have visited him in prison but she had not been able to bring herself to do it. What would there have been to say?

She thought he looked ill. His hands were manacled behind his back and there were chains on his ankles so that he could not run away. As if that would have been possible anyway.

At first he seemed to be looking at the ground, but then he lifted his head and appeared to be searching for someone in the crowd. She knew who that someone was, but she doubted whether he would see her. It might have been possible to catch his attention by raising her arm and waving, but she did not.

Nevertheless, as he drew level with the place where she was standing she thought that for a moment he might have caught a glimpse of her and that the faintest of smiles touched his lips. It was so momentary that she could not be certain that she had not imagined it. Then the chanting priest, a large fat man with a tonsured head, had gone by with the prisoner following.

He stumbled just before he reached the guillotine. They had to help him into the correct position, lying face downward, so that he was the only one there who could not see the blade that was to end his life. The crowd was silent now, as if for a moment it had lost its corporate voice.

She heard the rattle of the blade descending, but she did not see it reach the victim, for she had turned her head away. She heard a sound go up from the crowd; it was like the baying of some pack of wild beasts, inhuman. But she heard nothing more and saw nothing more. The entire scene had vanished from her consciousness.

She had fainted.

3

BELLA

Her name was Isabella Foster. To friends and relations she had always been known as Bella. There could not have been a more fitting name, for she was indeed beautiful. No one could have disputed the fact, and no one attempted to do so.

She had two younger sisters, quite pretty girls but not exceptional. She was.

Mr Foster was an ironmonger, and a prosperous one. A lean, hatchet-faced man who seldom smiled, he had a shop in a village a few miles south of Norwich and a large house adjoining it. To the rear of the shop was a range of outbuildings in which could be found a stock of hardware goods so comprehensive that few customers ever went away having failed to discover exactly what they required. From galvanised iron rainwater tanks of every size and shape to garden rakes and from scythes to table knives, all were there if you were prepared to seek them out. You could also have your horse shod if need be, for there was a smithy in an open-fronted shed nearby. Naturally Mr Foster himself did no such manual labour; he employed a smith named Arthur Hodges and a pimply apprentice who probably had a name but was always referred to as 'the boy'.

Henry Foster, having accumulated and invested a considerable amount of wealth, and with the prospect of gaining more every day, had certain aspirations towards raising himself and his family in the social scale. In this endeavour he was encouraged by his wife, Miriam, who had always felt that she had married rather beneath her when she agreed, after much hesitation, to become the wife of a village ironmonger.

Not that any unbiased person would have considered it much of a descent in the social pecking order for the daughter of a struggling tenant farmer with no more than a hundred acres of rather poor soil from which to scratch a living. But there it was; and if Mrs Foster had not brought much of a dowry with her she did at least possess certain physical attributes to pass on to her daughters, especially the eldest.

The girls themselves benefited by being sent as weekly boarders to a rather expensive private school run by a maiden lady of impeccable parentage but slender means. This school was some three miles east of Norwich and at weekends Foster himself would drive a pony and trap to bring the pupils home for the weekend.

At some extra charge Miss Lowther could arrange for any of her girls – there were no boys – to take dancing lessons from a master of the art named Gerald Hardacre, who came up by train from London twice a week for that purpose.

This gentleman, if such he could be called, was possibly thirty-five years old and had a certain raffish air about him. He had oiled black hair, side whiskers and a small moustache. There were rumours that he was related, whether closely or distantly could not be determined, to Miss Lowther. But if this were so, neither of them ever gave any indication that it was.

Another rumour had it that Hardacre was connected in some way with the stage. And this might have been true, though nobody could advance any hard evidence for it. When the weather was fine he would walk from Norwich to the school, stick in hand and hat tilted at a jaunty angle, the very picture of a debonair man-about-town. One thing about Gerald Hardacre that could not be denied was that he was an excellent dancing-master. And another thing was that Isabella Foster was his star pupil.

'You,' he once told her, 'have it in you. All I have to do is bring it out. And that is not in the least difficult.'

It helped, of course, that she loved dancing. With her it amounted almost to an obsession.

She was sixteen when he first hinted at the possibility of

a career on the stage. It had never occurred to her before, but now that he had put the idea into her head she could not help being fascinated by such a prospect. If only it could come true!

Yet she kept such thoughts to herself. She felt sure that her parents, especially her father, would never approve of such a thing. The stage! A dancer! It was unthinkable.

Moreover, after that initial hint Hardacre himself appeared to forget about it for a time. Certainly he did not mention it again and might perhaps have forgotten it; though she had not.

Months passed. It came into her mind now and then to broach the subject herself; to ask him whether he had been serious when he made that suggestion regarding a career on the stage. But she feared he might laugh and say that he had only been joking. So she said nothing.

Almost a year went by. She was seventeen now and would soon be leaving Miss Lowther's establishment. What she would do then was a question that had never been discussed. What did young ladies in her position do? Help their mothers with household duties; go to balls and parties while waiting for a suitable young man to make an offer of marriage? It all seemed so vague.

Then, quite out of the blue, Gerald Hardacre said: 'Well? Have you thought about it?'

She knew at once what he was referring to, though all

those months had passed and there had not been so much as a hint that it was still in his mind. Now she realised that, far from forgetting the suggestion he had made, he had simply been biding his time, letting the idea take root, as it were, in her mind until the moment seemed right to repeat it.

Adroitly now he had managed matters so that they were alone together, and he spoke with some urgency.

'Of course you have. And it's what you want, isn't it? Don't deny it. I can see it in your eyes. And I can arrange everything. All you need to say is yes.'

But still she hesitated. It was such a big step to take; leaving home and putting her trust in a man about whom she really knew so little. So for a time she resisted his blandishments even though her inclination was to give in and follow the dream.

Oddly enough it was her father himself who caused her to make the fateful decision. They had an argument over some trivial matter which she could never afterwards remember, even though it was to prove of such consequence to her future existence. The man had lost his patience and in a fit of temper had slapped her on the cheek.

It was no gentle slap; it really stung and brought tears to her eyes. Moreover, it was so unexpected, for he was not a man who habitually resorted to physical violence. Indeed, he regretted it at once and felt an urge to apologise, perhaps even to beg for her forgiveness, but he hesitated, and then it was too late.

'Beast!' she said. And the look she gave him was of such bitterness that it quite took him aback.

Then she turned and ran from the room. In that moment, though he did not realise it at the time, and indeed could not have guessed such a thing, he had lost a daughter.

For the rest of the weekend relations between the two of them were strained. Though neither of them made any reference to the incident, neither of them had forgotten it. Mrs Foster could not help noticing that something was amiss, but she refrained from making any remark. If either husband or daughter felt inclined to confide in her she was willing to listen to what they had to say, but it was up to them to make the approach; and as neither appeared inclined to do so she said nothing.

Then on the Monday morning the girls went back to school, and on his appointed day Gerald Hardacre came up from London to instruct the young ladies in the art of dancing. For Isabella Foster it was to be a visit that would have the most profound effect, for good or bad, on the future course of her life.

If anyone noticed that she and the dancing master had a rather lengthy discussion with each other when the lesson was over, no one mentioned it. Perhaps it was not even remarked, for Hardacre and Miss Foster had become adept at avoiding observation when they had their tête-à-tête discussions, and on this occasion, although the business might have taken rather longer than usual, it was, if observed at all, probably regarded as no more than some exchange of views concerning the dance routine that had just been completed. Certainly no one could have guessed that some much more serious matter was being discussed, and indeed that certain plans were being laid that for one at least of the pair would effect the most complete change to her way of life that could be imagined.

'So,' the man said, putting a hand on the girl's arm, 'you are quite sure this is what you want to do?'

It was almost as if, now that she had at last agreed to do what he had for so long urged upon her, he was himself having doubts regarding the wisdom of the move. Perhaps some trace of better nature, a touch of conscience, had hinted to him that he was taking advantage of the inexperience of an innocent young girl and maybe ruining her prospects in life.

But then she answered: 'Yes. Oh, yes. Of course it is.' And he suppressed those slight feelings of guilt and even convinced himself that what he was doing was for her benefit rather than his own. For was he not putting her on the path to a glittering career in the sphere that she yearned to enter? What could possibly be wrong with that?

So it was settled.

'You will never regret this,' he said.

And hoped that it might be true.

4

DEPARTURE

It happened at the weekend. To be more precise, it was the Sunday; eleven p.m. or a little later.

The Foster household was not in the habit of staying up late. After all, what was there to stay up for? It was simply a waste of fuel now that the autumn weather was becoming daily more like winter. So at eleven o'clock all were in bed and almost certainly sound asleep.

All, that is, with one exception: Isabella.

She was certainly not asleep. She was not even in bed, but was fully clothed and required no more than an over-coat and a hat to be ready to leave the house. Moreover, there was beside the bed a kind of trunk which consisted of two basketwork halves, one fitting into the other and secured by straps. This trunk appeared to be extended to its maximum capacity and it would certainly not have been possible to squeeze anything more into it.

Isabella, as the oldest girl in the Foster family, had a

bedroom to herself; the two younger sisters sharing another. This was fortunate, since otherwise the operation planned for that night would not have been possible. Even as it was she waited on tenterhooks, fearing that something might go wrong. Suppose one of those sisters should wake and hear a suspicious noise. She knew it was most unlikely, for girls of that age slept like logs and took a deal of waking; but there was nonetheless a faint possibility that it might happen.

Fortunately too, her parents' bedroom was some distance away on the opposite side of the landing from which the stairs descended to the entrance hall. There was yet another bedroom in which the housemaid or skivvy slept, but this was an attic and it was unlikely that anything would wake that young person before the alarm-clock went off at the appointed hour of six a.m., when she would rise and start on her daily round of labour.

Isabella shivered. It was chilly in the bedroom. The flame of the candle which was the sole illumination flickered, revealing that there was a draught somewhere, and it threw dancing shadows on the flowery wallpaper. A cheap tin clock on the dressing-table ticked away the seconds, and she kept glancing at it and thinking how slowly time was passing.

Suppose, she thought, he did not come. Suppose he had changed his mind or had never intended going through with the scheme. Suppose he had simply been playing a game with her; making a fool of her while all the time he had been laughing up his sleeve.

She almost came to believe this as she watched the guttering candle drip winding-sheets down its steadily diminishing length. Little pools of molten wax formed and hardened in the candlestick and the clock ticked on.

And then she heard it: a faint brushing sound coming from the window, possibly made by a small branch that had been plucked from a bush or garden hedge and was now being moved from side to side on the glass.

It galvanised her at once. She picked up the candlestick, carried it to the window and pulled one of the curtains aside to allow a sliver of light to escape for a moment before returning it to its former position.

Wasting no time now, she put on her hat and coat, took the candle to the door and opened it with great care to make as little sound as possible. With the candlestick still in her hand she tiptoed to the head of the stairs and set it down in such a position that it shed some light on the staircase.

There was now very little light in her bedroom, but she knew exactly where the trunk was, and she picked it up and carried it out of the room. She set it down for a moment so that she could close the bedroom door, then picked it up and carried it to the head of the stairs. It would have saved time if she could have carried both candlestick and trunk down the stairs together, but this was not possible. So she took the candlestick first, set it down near the front door and then returned for the trunk.

The door was a stout one, made of oak, and there were iron bolts at the top and bottom as well as a lock with a massive key which was hanging on a nail in the wall on the right.

Having set down the trunk, Isabella proceeded to draw back the bolts, and since they had not been greased for some time this was an operation that could not be completed without a certain amount of noise. To the girl, whose nerves were already somewhat jangled, it sounded loud enough to rouse all the sleepers in the house, and her hand shook as she reached for the key.

She had never before had any reason to lock or unlock the door and she was surprised to discover how difficult an operation it was. She tried first with one hand but could not move the key; it was as though it were solidly imbedded in the lock, and the sickening thought came to her that, after all the meticulous preparation she had made, all might yet be brought to nothing by so small a thing as the failure to turn a key.

In desperation she grasped the key with both hands and tried again. Still it resisted. She was almost weeping with frustration, but she gave a last twist to the key, and it hurt her fingers but the key gave way with an unpleasant grinding sound and turned in the lock. She lifted the latch and pulled the door open.

Immediately a gust of cold air came in and blew the candle out.

She heard a man's voice. 'So there you are. I thought you were never coming.'

There was a trace of peevishness in the tone, as though he resented having been kept waiting.

She could see him only as a shadowy figure, for there was no moon and none of the houses in the street was showing any light. A few stars were visible through breaks in the clouds but that was all.

'I had trouble with the lock,' she said. 'It was so stiff.'

'Well you're here now. Have you got your luggage?'

'Yes, it's here.'

She picked up the trunk and carried it over the doorstep.

'Give me that,' he said, taking it from her. 'Shut the door.'

She did so as silently as she could, though still the sound of it seemed to her loud enough to rouse everyone in the house.

'Now,' Hardacre said, 'let's be on our way.'

He set off up the street with the trunk on his shoulder and she followed, trotting to keep up with him, her heart beating like a wild thing now that she was breaking away from all that life had previously held for her and was heading into the unknown like a mariner sailing into uncharted seas.

The horse and gig were at the end of the street, and she caught the scent of the driver's pipe before she could see him. The gig had lamps with candles in them which would give warning to any other road users at that time of night that the gig was there but revealed little of the road ahead to the driver.

The man with the pipe had a hat pulled down over his ears and a muffler round his neck, so that, even if there had been more light, it would have been difficult to make out much of his face. It was obvious that there had to be a pipe stuck in his mouth, but only the occasional faint glow from this gave evidence of its whereabouts. He said nothing when Hardacre arrived with the girl, though he might have thought a lot. He was probably being well paid for his services so late at night and had been told as little regarding the true nature of what was afoot as was essential. Possibly he did not wish to know more.

Hardacre stowed the trunk in the gig and helped Isabella to follow it in, using the step on the near side. Then he followed, guided her to a seat and sat down beside her. Having done so he gave a word to the driver to be on his way.

The man cracked his whip and the horse responded, the iron-bound wheels grating on the stones in the road.

Isabella shivered, not only from the chill in the air but also from the thought that this really was a step which could not be retracted. It was all so different, this nocturnal ride in a gig which had almost certainly been previously used for the transport of pigs, from those other rides in the pony-trap driven by her father.

The thought came to her that she might never again see the ironmonger's shop and the smithy and Ben, the blacksmith with his massive arms and ready smile; and again she gave a shiver.

'Cold?' Hardacre asked.

'A little.'

'Well, it won't be long now.'

He did not say what would not be long and she did not ask.

5

HOME

They reached the station at Norwich in less than half an hour. Hardacre paid the driver of the gig and without a word he turned it in the forecourt and drove away. Isabella had caught no more than a glimpse of his face in the gloom and she doubted whether she would recognise him if she ever saw him again.

'Come along then,' Hardacre said.

He was carrying the trunk and led the way through the entrance to the station. This was a poorly lit and depressing kind of place at that time of night and there was not a great deal of activity in evidence. There was a waiting-room lit by one gas-lamp and some cinders in a fireplace gave evidence that a fire had been burning in it earlier. Now that it had gone out the room was decidedly chilly. The furniture comprised of some bare wooden benches and a table.

'Hardly luxurious,' Hardacre said. 'But at least we've got

it to ourselves and we must make the best of it for a while,
I'm afraid.'

He dumped the trunk on a seat and guided Isabella with
a hand on her arm. She sat down and he took his place
beside her. He took a watch from his pocket and consulted it.

'By my reckoning,' he said, 'we have possibly six hours to
wait. We could have gone to an inn or hotel, but that might
have made us conspicuous. Don't want to draw attention to
ourselves, do we?'

'You mean we are to wait in here until morning?'

'That's it. You don't object to some slight hardship for a
start, do you? It's in a good cause.'

He had not mentioned this when he had sketched his
plan for her and she had never questioned him closely. She
had put her trust in him. He was a man of the world and
surely knew the best course to take. Besides, what did a
little initial discomfort matter if it was to lead to something
so desirable?

'No,' she said, 'I don't mind.'

She did not think she could possibly sleep in such condi-
tions, but in the event she did. She woke to find the man's
arms around her and her head resting on his chest. She
drew away from him almost violently.

He gave a chuckle. 'Ah, I see you're awake. I hope you've
had a good refreshing sleep.'

'How long—' she said, and stopped.

'How long have you been asleep? Oh, a few hours. I didn't

like to wake you. After all, it's passed the time, hasn't it? For you at least.'

There was still no daylight, and it seemed to be even colder in the waiting-room.

'Our train leaves at six o'clock. That will give us time for an early breakfast.'

'Breakfast?'

'You sound surprised. My dear Miss Foster, surely you didn't imagine I would be so improvident as to neglect our bodily needs. Never.'

There was a haversack lying on the seat. She had noticed he was carrying it when they set out but had not remarked on it. Now he took from it some slices of bread and cheese wrapped in paper. There were also two bottles with screw stoppers.

'Beer for me,' he said, 'and lemonade for the lady. No tea or coffee, I'm afraid, but one cannot have everything in circumstances such as these.'

Although it was much earlier than her normal breakfast time she discovered that she was quite hungry. She would have preferred a hot drink to the cold lemonade, but there was no way the man could have brought a teapot or a pot of steaming coffee with him.

'What time is it now?' she asked after they had finished their meal.

He again fished up the watch on its chain from his waist-coat pocket and consulted it.

'It's a quarter past five,' he said. 'We haven't very much longer to wait. How are you feeling on this bright and shining morning.'

Rather to her own surprise she felt remarkably well after her brief sleep and the makeshift breakfast. Even the chill in the bleak waiting-room did not bother her. She was wearing a winter coat which reached down to her laced-up boots, and really she did not feel uncomfortably cold.

She wondered what was happening in the house she had left so secretly. She felt quite sure her absence would not yet have been discovered. Even the skivvy would not be up and about to begin her daily chores just yet; and even when she did there was no likelihood of her discovering the absence of Miss Isabella from her bedroom. She would probably be the first to notice the candlestick in the hall and then catch sight of the bolts on the front door and the key in the lock. But that would not be for some time yet, and when the discovery was made she and Gerald would already be on their way to London.

London! At the thought of it excitement bubbled up in her. That famous city was where her future lay. That was where she would make her name and fortune. She was sure of it. She had to be.

At the start of the journey they had a compartment to themselves, and the train had scarcely left the station when Isabella had a surprise: Hardacre flung his arms round her and kissed her on the lips.

It was utterly unexpected and also such a new experience. Hitherto the only kisses she had received had been little pecks from parents and aunts and the occasional pouting touch from some shy boy at a birthday or Christmas party. This kiss from Gerald Hardacre was of a different character altogether, and her initial reaction was one of shock. She made an effort to draw away from him, but this was difficult, if not completely impossible, since she was sitting at one end of the seat and was trapped between the man and the window of the compartment. She said nothing. Indeed, it would hardly have been possible to utter a word with the man's mouth glued to hers as if with some strong adhesive. Moreover, after the initial shock of this totally unexpected embrace had passed she discovered that she did not altogether dislike the experience and that it was really quite enjoyable.

Then he released her and remarked, as though the kiss had been of no consequence and was not worth mentioning: 'These carriages are very cold, don't you think? I suppose some day they'll find a way of heating them.'

'Yes,' she said, 'I suppose they will.' And though she tried to speak naturally she could not quite manage it. There was a slight tremor in her voice which betrayed the fact that she was still feeling the effect of that sudden embrace.

*

The train was a slow one. It stopped at all the small stations along the line and at several of them large churns of milk were put on board. At each station more passengers joined the train and long before they reached their journey's end the compartment was full.

Isabella could tell when they were nearing the Metropolis because there were more buildings on each side; some of them houses, rows and rows of them, and others which she took to be factories with tall chimneys belching out smoke. The train slowed; now and then it came to a halt for some reason before going on again. None of the other passengers appeared to be at all concerned about this stopping and starting, so she concluded that it was normal procedure. They passed under some bridges and she could see from the window that there were several other railway lines. Then the train slowed even more and finally came to a halt under a high glazed roof.

'Well,' Hardacre said, 'here we are. London town.'

Someone had opened the door on the side where the platform was and people were leaving the compartment. Hardacre allowed them all to go before taking the girl's trunk from the luggage rack.

'Now let's go.'

Her first impression was of noise and activity. There was also a rather acrid odour which might have come from the

46

engine, a mixture of steam and smoke. There were porters here and there with trolleys, others carrying hand luggage. One of these offered his services to Hardacre but was repulsed.

'I think,' he said, 'we should get something to eat. It's a long time since we had breakfast. Are you hungry?'

In fact she was feeling too excited to be aware of hunger, but she allowed him to guide her to a refreshment room where they had coffee and buttered rolls.

'And now,' Hardacre said after they had finished this light meal, 'we may as well go home.'

Home! Perhaps it was this word that fully impressed upon her the inescapable reality of the step she had taken. In the past home had meant nothing else but the house adjoining the ironmonger's shop and the smithy. Now it signified something else altogether; a place she had not yet set eyes on.

It was not a great way from Liverpool Street station. They could have walked it if it had not been for the girl's trunk. As it was, they took a cab and came very soon to a cul-de-sac with a row of houses on each side, the front doors of which opened directly on to the pavement.

Hardacre paid off the cabbie and carried the trunk to one of these doors, where he set it down and took a key from his jacket pocket. He unlocked the door, opened it and invited the girl to go inside. She did so and found herself, not in any entrance hall but in what was evidently the front room of the house. It was small and the well-worn sofa and two armchairs that constituted the main furniture occupied most of the space. There was a threadbare carpet on the floor, a fireplace with some dead cinders in it, a junk-loaded mantelpiece and a cracked mirror above. The dingy wall-paper was peeling away in places and some of the plaster had fallen from the ceiling.

The sight of this room came as an unpleasant shock to the girl. She could not have said precisely what she had been expecting, but certainly it had been nothing like this. She would never have imagined that a man as debonair as Gerald Hardacre would be living in a place like this. It would have been inconceivable.

He must have guessed what was in her mind; must have been aware of the unpleasant impression the sight of this room had made on her; for he said quickly:

'This is only rented, you know. Just a pied-à-terre until I find something more suitable. And you'll find it's quite cosy when we get the fire going.'

'Yes,' she said, 'I'm sure it will.'

But there was doubt in her mind.

He made haste to show her the rest of the house, as if to get the whole unpleasant business over and done with as quickly as possible. There was a kitchen with a washhouse adjoining it and a backyard with walls on each side to sepa-rate it from the neighbours. A rather narrow staircase led to a small landing and two bedrooms, the larger of which was furnished with a double bed and the smaller with a single bed.

Hardacre carried the girl's luggage up the stairs and into the smaller bedroom.

'There's some bed-linen in the cupboard,' he said. 'We can air it when I've lit the fires.'

He set about this task at once. There was coal and kindling in an outhouse, and he soon had fires going in the kitchen and the front room. She was surprised to see how adept he was at these tasks, but she supposed that, living alone, he had to do things for himself. There was no skivvy in this house. Soon there were sheets and blankets draped over chairs in front of both fires and the house was beginning to feel much warmer.

'There's a corner shop down the road,' he said. 'We can get provisions there. And there's a bakery not far off. Are you any good at cooking?'

'I've done a bit,' she said. 'My mother taught me. At weekends.'

'Well, that's fine.' He gave a grin. 'I can see that we're not going to starve.'

She noticed that he had made no mention yet of the stage, but of course there would be time for that later. No doubt he would tell what his plans were as soon as he had worked things out. She decided not to press him on that subject yet. It was enough for the present that she had broken the ties that had bound her to the family and all the petty restrictions of her former way of life. Now she was free to follow her own inclination without restraint or criticism.

Yes, without doubt she had done the right thing.

And if she had not it was too late to turn back.

6

CONFRONTATION

Two weeks passed and the main change that had taken place in the domestic arrangements was that she was sleeping with Gerald Hardacre.

She supposed that some people, indeed possibly most people, might have said that a man of the world had seduced a young and inexperienced girl. But the fact was that she had been only too willing, even eager, to be seduced.

She was in love with him; or imagined she was. Perhaps really she was in love with love. And no one could deny that Hardacre was a charming and handsome man; the kind that anyone might fall for. Moreover, sharing a comfortable double bed was certainly preferable to sleeping alone on an iron single bed with a hard mattress and springs that gave a metallic twang whenever one moved.

'I've told the neighbours you're my sister come to keep house for me,' Hardacre said. 'Don't want to set tongues wagging, do we? People do so love to pass scandal around.

Not that I mind for myself, of course. They can say what they like about me. Water off a duck's back and all that. But we don't want a lot of tittle-tattle about you, my dear, do we?'

He had started putting out feelers, so he said. By which she understood that he was approaching theatre managements, though he did not say as much. She wondered why he did not take her with him; but perhaps that would come later. As he remarked, Rome was not built in a day.

It was one of those days when he had left her alone in the house that there came a knock at the front door. This was unusual; in fact it was unique. In the couple of weeks she had spent in the house no one at all had called. The postman had pushed one or two letters through the letter-box, but these had been for Hardacre and were of no importance, at least, so he had assured her. But until now no one had knocked on the door, and she wondered who it could be. It could hardly be someone calling to see her, since no one except the neighbours knew she was living there.

At first she made no move to the door and rather hoped that the unseen caller would conclude that there was no one at home and go away.

But this was not to be. Another knock sounded rather louder than the first, as though the person outside were determined not to be put off.

Isabella decided to see who it was. She unlocked the door and pulled it open. There was a man standing on the doorstep and he spoke rather testily.

'So there you are at last. I was beginning to think you'd decided to keep me out.'

She saw with a sinking heart that it was her father; and she also saw that he was not in the best of tempers.

'Well,' he said, 'now that you've condescended to open the door aren't you going to invite me in?'

She guessed that he needed no invitation. The only way she could have kept him out would have been to slam the door in his face, and she could not bring herself to do that.

So she said: 'Well, I suppose now that you're here you'd better come inside.'

'Hardly the most gracious of invitations,' he said, 'but I'll accept it.'

He walked past her and she closed the door, wondering as she did so how he had discovered the address. He had taken off his hat and was casting a glance round the room with an expression of distaste, but he made no comment on it.

'Where's that scoundrel?' he demanded.

She answered with some asperity: 'If you mean Mr Hardacre he's not at home. And he's not a scoundrel.'

'That's a matter of opinion. But perhaps it's as well he's not here. I might have given him a sound thrashing.'

He had a walking-stick with him and he made a few passes with it as if to demonstrate what he might have done to the scoundrel if the fellow had been within reach.

'Now Pa,' she said, 'do calm down. Let me make you a cup of tea.'

'Tea!' He made it sound as if she had offered him a draught of prussic acid, but he did calm down enough to let her take his hat and coat and persuade him to sit down in one of the much-used armchairs.

'How did you find me?' she asked.

'Ah!' he said. 'Wouldn't you like to know?'

But he did not tell her, and she wondered just why it had taken so long.

7

SHOCK FOR MISS LOWTHER

The fact of the matter was that on the Monday morning after her departure the first intimation that anything was amiss in the ironmonger's household was given by the skivvy. She had been up and about for some time, raking out grates and lighting fires and attending to other duties, before she noticed the candlestick on the floor by the front door. It had puzzled her, but even when she had also observed that the bolts on the door had been slid back and that the key had been turned in the lock the full import of these facts did not strike her immediately. It was not until Mr Foster got up and she reported this odd fact to him that suspicions that something was very much amiss began to be aroused.

Still, however, it did not occur to the good man that one of his daughters might have made a nocturnal flight from the family home. What possible reason could there have been for any one of them to escape from a house where they had everything that a young lady could desire? It was unthinkable.

Not until the absence of Isabella from the breakfast table did the suspicion that all was not well in the Foster ménage begin to be entertained.

Then, of course, it took no more than a hasty visit to that young person's bedroom to confirm their worst suspicions.

There was a note left on the dressing-table. It was brief and to the point.

'When you read this I shall be far away. Do not try to follow me. I shall not come back. Love, Bella.'

Mr Foster was enraged. Mrs Foster was distraught. The two younger daughters were thrilled. The skivvy was envious.

When they had recovered from the initial shock Mr and Mrs Foster had a discussion regarding what had better be done. The girls were not initially consulted.

'There must be some man involved in this,' Foster said. 'She wouldn't run away by herself.'

'But she doesn't know any men, does she?'

'Not to our knowledge.'

'Where on earth can she have gone?'

'Goodness knows.'

'Do you think we ought to go to the police?'

'The police!' Mr Foster was aghast. 'Do you want

everyone to know that our daughter has run away? Think of the gossip that would cause.'

'But what are we to tell people? Miss Lowther for instance when you take the other girls to school.'

Foster had to admit that this was a problem. 'I shall tell her that she is indisposed.'

'But Jenny and Paula know she's run away. Won't they talk about it to the other girls?'

'We must give them strict instructions not to mention it to anyone.'

Mrs Foster looked doubtful. She was not at all sure her younger daughters could be relied on to keep such a secret to themselves when they were with their friends at school, but she could think of no reasonable alternative. The maidservant of course would be ordered not to breathe a word regarding the matter to anyone, and she could be relied on to keep a still tongue in her head because there was a threat of instant dismissal if she did not.

So a week passed. Mr Foster went to fetch his daughters from school and assured Miss Lowther that Isabella was progressing as well as could be expected, but they might send her to stay with an aunt in Brighton to recuperate.

'The sea air should be good for her.'

Miss Lowther said she hoped it would have the desired effect; but Mr Foster thought she had a rather worried look, as though there was something on her mind; but he supposed the running of a private boarding school for young ladies was bound to be a somewhat worrying business. It did not occur to him that Miss Lowther's worries could have any connection with his own, but at that time he had no reason to suppose they had.

Another week passed and the two Foster girls were home again for the weekend. Nothing had been heard from Isabella and they still had no idea where she had gone. Then, quite unexpectedly there came a breakthrough, or at least the possibility of one. The Foster family had just finished their midday meal when Jenny said:

'Paula and I think we know who Bell's run off with.'

Both parents stared at her.

'Are you serious?' Mr Foster demanded.

'Dead serious.'

'Then who do you think it is?'

'Mr Hardacre.'

'The dancing-master?'

'She's always been sweet on him,' Paula said. 'Talking to him in corners when they thought nobody saw them and all that.'

'And now,' Jenny said, 'he's stopped coming.'

'What do you mean – stopped coming?'

'Hasn't been seen these last two weeks. Dancing classes cancelled. Miss L says Mr H is indisposed, like Bella. But we don't believe that either. You can see she's bothered. He's her nephew, you know.'

'Who told you that?'

'Oh, it's common knowledge among the girls, though she's never admitted it.'

It was the end of his day of rest for Mr Foster. He put on his hat and coat, harnessed the pony to the trap and set off at once to pay a call on Miss Lowther.

He could tell by the expression on her face that she had guessed the purpose of his visit as soon as she saw him. She took him into her private room and closed the door.

'Pray sit down, Mr Foster. Perhaps you would care for a cup of tea?'

He sat down. 'No tea, thank you, Miss Lowther. The fact is I have had some information that rather disturbs me.'

'Information, Mr Foster?'

'Concerning my daughter Isabella.'

'Isabella? But is she not in Brighton?'

'Brighton? Oh, no. I don't think we need keep up that pretence any longer. I think we both know she never went to Brighton, don't we?'

Miss Lowther said nothing. She waited for her visitor to continue, and after a brief pause he did so.

'She has run away.'

'Run away, Mr Foster?'

'Run away, Miss Lowther. Run away with, so I am led to believe, your dancing-master.'

Miss Lowther raised her hands in horror. 'My dancing-master! Surely not. I cannot believe such a thing. No. It is quite impossible.'

'I only wish it was,' Foster said. 'Nothing would please me more than to be assured that such a thing was impossible. But tell me, Miss Lowther, when was the man last here to give instruction to the young ladies?'

Miss Lowther made no immediate reply. She seemed to be trying hard to think of some answer that might not be a lie and yet might also not be an admission that Gerald Hardacre had not been seen by her for the past fortnight. And as there was no way of doing this she remained silent.

Mr Foster prompted her again. 'This man. What is his name?'

Miss Lowther found her tongue, though with some apparent reluctance, as if she were aware that she was allowing a breach to be made in her defences.

'Gerald Hardacre.'

Mr Foster repeated the name with some apparent distaste. 'Gerald Hardacre. And would I be correct in suggesting that he is a relation of yours?'

Miss Lowther, having conceded one point, apparently could see no alternative but to concede another, even if it did appear to stick in her throat.

'He is my nephew.'

And at this moment she was sincerely wishing she had never obliged the young man by offering him employment when he was resting, as it was termed in the profession to which he belonged. She had even paid him a good deal more than she would have had to pay any other dancing-master simply out of the kindness of her heart in dealing with a near relation. And this was how her generosity had been rewarded. He had brought shame on the school, and if word of the sorry business came to the ears of her pupils' parents, as it inevitably would, there was no telling how many of them might decide to remove their little darlings from such undesirable influences as were apparently present in that establishment.

Miss Lowther saw ruin staring her in the face and her only hope was that Mr Foster would be just as keen as she was to repress the scandal. Of course she had always known that Gerald was a young man with a certain, not altogether desirable reputation, and she might have been warned by this that it would be unwise to place him in the company of a number of impressionable young ladies. But who would have imagined that he would have run off with one of them? And she no more than seventeen years old.

'Ah!' Mr Foster said. 'Your nephew, is he? And are you going to tell me that you had no knowledge of what kind of character he had?'

Miss Lowther made no reply to this.

'A nice sort of person, I must say, to let loose among a company of defenceless young girls.'

Mr Foster made it sound like a wolf being wilfully introduced to a flock of sheep. Which was perhaps how he regarded it.

'I shall require his address, of course. I assume you have it.'

Miss Lowther thought for a moment of denying that she had such knowledge. But she knew that he would not believe her. And how would it have helped anyway? So she went to her davenport desk, opened it and wrote on a slip of paper which she then handed to her visitor.

'What do you intend to do?'

'Intend to do! What do you think? I shall do my duty as a responsible parent. I shall go and bring my daughter home. By force if necessary.'

He did not explain just what he meant by force. Perhaps he himself did not know precisely. Miss Lowther had visions of him putting a rope round the girl's neck and dragging her through the streets. She wondered just how Gerald would react. Would it come to a bout of fisticuffs between him and the irate father? Foster was a well-built man and perhaps would use a walking-stick on Gerald's shoulders. A good thing if he did perhaps. It might teach the young fellow a lesson. Though much good that would do now.

When he went back to his pony-trap Foster left Miss Lowther a very troubled woman, uncertain of what the future might hold for her and her school. But there was nothing she could do to change matters. She could only wait and hope for the best while fearing the worst.

8

WASTED JOURNEY

Sitting in the sagging armchair, Mr Foster made an examination of the room, his expression one of distaste.

'I hardly expected a daughter of mine,' he said, 'to exchange the drawing-room in my house for a place like this. Doesn't it sicken you?'

'Not at all,' she said. 'And of course it's only temporary. We'll soon be moving into somewhere much better.'

She had no grounds for this assertion apart from Hardacre's statement that this was merely a pied-à-terre until he found something more suitable. But two weeks had passed since then and he had said nothing more on that subject.

She was not sure what he did when he went out alone, sometimes for nearly the whole of the day. He said he was still making inquiries and doing some groundwork, whatever that was. Only to herself did she admit to a feeling of some uneasiness. When urging her to come away with him he had given the impression that there was a career on the stage just waiting for her in London and that he had influence in the right quarters to get things moving. But it had all seemed rather vague, and to date nothing had moved as far as she could see.

Then there was the question of money. She was not sure how much he had, but she doubted whether it was enough to last for long. She herself had none, and living on air was no more feasible in the Metropolis than it was in the country; perhaps even less so. The air was certainly more polluted.

Her father had finally accepted a cup of tea and some biscuits. She wondered when he had last had a meal. Perhaps he was really hungry.

She asked him again how he had discovered where she was living, and this time he told her the whole story. So it had been her dear little sisters who had given the game away. She supposed that was only to be expected. They would have been delighted to do so.

'Miss Lowther is most upset,' Foster said.

'I don't see why she should be.'

'You don't see? Why, isn't it obvious that if the story gets handed round it could harm the reputation of her school? And it will get round. These things always do. Of course she's regretting now that she ever employed her nephew as a dancing-master.'

'Her nephew? Are you saying Gerald is Miss Lowther's nephew?'

'Certainly. Didn't you know?'

She had not known. He had never mentioned the relationship. But perhaps he had assumed that she was already aware of the fact. Not that it made any difference to the situation of course.

Mr Foster took another sip of tea and looked at his erring daughter over the rim of the cup. She looked back at him and noticed how much grey there was in his hair. She had never taken much note of it before, and the thought occurred to her that perhaps he would blame her for turning his hair grey by the worry that her conduct had caused him. The idea made her smile. It was so ludicrous.

He noticed the smile and reacted at once.

'I suppose you think this is very funny.'

'No, Pa, not at all. And I'm sorry to have put you to the bother of making such a long journey for nothing.'

'You think it's been for nothing?'

'Well, hasn't it?'

'Not at all. I came to take you back to where you belong. And that's what I intend to do. You'd better start packing your things at once.'

'No, Pa.'

'What do you mean? No, Pa. Are you defying me?'

'Yes, I suppose I am.'

Mr Foster put down his teacup and moved forward to the edge of the chair. 'Now see here, my girl, you are in no position to disobey me. You are still a minor and subject to my authority. I have the law on my side, and though I should be reluctant to have recourse to it, if there is no alternative I may have to.'

'My goodness, Pa. Are you threatening to fetch a policeman and take me away in handcuffs?'

Mr Foster went quite red in the face. 'Oh, you may think it's all a joke, but I assure you it's not. And as for that young man, he could find himself in jail, you know. Abducting a minor is a criminal offence, and so he would very soon find out.'

Isabella stared at him. 'You would never do it.'

'Oh, indeed! And why wouldn't I?'

'You've been talking about the scandal, but what scandal could be worse than that? My goodness, there would be some tongue-wagging then, wouldn't there? And how they'd all love it.'

And suddenly he broke down. He buried his face in his hands and she could see his shoulders quivering. Strange little sounds were coming from him and she realised that he was weeping.

She was shocked. It was so unlike him. She would never have suspected any such weakness in him. She put a hand on his shoulder.

'Don't, Pa, don't.'

Without looking up he started mumbling: 'You were always my favourite, you know.'

She did not know. As far as she could remember he had

never shown any affection for any of his children. He had been kind but strict. Perhaps he had been reluctant to show any emotion. Well, he was showing it now.

He lifted his head and she could see the tears in his eyes. It embarrassed her and she could think of nothing to say.

'My lovely Bella,' he said. 'You are so beautiful, and now it seems I've lost you.'

It was an admission of defeat. He knew that when he left the house he would go alone. And a little later he took his leave.

He had to come back a moment later because he had forgotten his walking-stick. Even as an anticlimax it was hardly one of the best.

It was two hours later when Hardacre walked in. Isabella told him at once:

'Pa has been.'

'Your father! Here! What did he want?'

'What do you think he wanted? To take me back with him, of course.'

'And of course you refused.'

'Well, I'm still here, aren't I?'

'How did he find out where you were living?'

'Miss Lowther told him.'

'But I don't understand. Why did he go to her?'

'Because my dear little sisters told him I'd run away with you.'

'Ah!'

'You didn't tell me she was your aunt.'

'Miss Lowther? Didn't I?'

'You know you didn't.'

'Well, maybe not. But it makes no difference, does it?'

'I suppose not. There's another thing, though. Pa said that if he called the police in you could be arrested and sent to jail for abducting a minor.'

Hardacre looked concerned at this. 'He wouldn't do it, would he?'

She could see that the possibility that her father might resort to such drastic measures to get his daughter back had scared him. Perhaps it had never entered his head when he was persuading her to go away with him that he might be committing a felony. Now the possible consequences of his action must have struck him for the first time, and he had turned quite pale.

Isabella mischievously allowed him to contemplate the awful possibility of arrest and imprisonment for a few moments before easing his mind.

Then she gave a laugh. 'Of course he wouldn't. Think of all the publicity there'd be. His name in the papers and everybody talking about it. He wouldn't want that. No, you can be sure he won't bring in the law to get me back. In fact he's given up trying. It's depressed him awfully. Said I'd always been his favourite daughter, which was news to me. In the end he really broke down. I never dreamed he'd be quite so upset about it. I felt more than a little sorry for him.'

'But it didn't make you change your mind.'

'Certainly not. For better or worse I've thrown in my lot with you, and nothing can alter that now. And you needn't worry about that threat of his. He won't do anything.'

Hardacre looked relieved, and she guessed that for a while he had imagined a policeman's hand on his shoulder and the sound of a key turning in a lock.

Then, as if casting all such gloomy thoughts aside, he said more cheerfully: 'I've news for you. Tomorrow morning we go to see a man named Walter Gage. So put on your best bib and tucker because we've got to impress him.'

'Who's Walter Gage?'

'Walter,' Hardacre said, 'is a man who could be the one to put us on the road to riches. Or, if not quite riches, at least to a decent income.'

Which did not tell her much. But he refused to say more. However, she had a feeling that something might be about to happen at last.

9

GATEWAY TO SUCCESS

It was the first time Miss Foster had ever entered a
theatre by way of the stage door. Indeed, she had
seldom been inside a theatre at all. When she had it was
to see a pantomime in Norwich in the Christmas holiday.
This was quite a different experience. The stage door was
in a rather dingy side-street, and when Hardacre pushed
it open and led the way inside they went into a kind of
lobby with what appeared to be a small office on the right
where a man in shirt-sleeves was doing some clerical
work.

Hardacre appeared to know the man and spoke to him
through a hatch in a glass window.

'Good morning, Alf. The guv'nor in?'

'Couldn't say, Mr Hardacre. You better go and see for
yourself. You know the way.'

'I should,' Hardacre said. 'Come along, Bella.'

He led the way and she followed, her heart beating faster

than usual with the realisation that she was in that part of a theatre which an audience never saw. They went past some dressing-rooms, the doors all shut, where a lingering suggestion of perfume and powder and bodily secretions hung on the still air as if waiting to greet the returning artistes later in the day.

They went up a stairway, a bare brick wall on one side, and found themselves at last in the wings of the stage. The curtain was up, and when they came out of the wings Isabella could see the dimly lit auditorium with the galleries and boxes higher up.

There were two men on the stage that appeared to be in conference. They were a complete contrast to each other. One was fat, squat and bald-headed, with a face that by its fiery appearance and its bulbous red nose gave evidence of a certain love of the bottle. The other was lean and lanky, with prominent cheekbones and a long, thin neck. He had a gloomy expression, as though he found nothing much in life to give him any pleasure.

Hardacre addressed the fat man. 'Good morning, Mr Gage.'

Gage turned and said in a husky voice which gave the impression that his words had been dredged up from somewhere deep in his throat: 'Ah, there you are, Mr Haitch. Brought the young lady, I see. Morning, Miss.'

He was giving her a very keen look and she felt slightly uncomfortable under the gaze. It was, she thought, as if he were seeing clean through her clothes and examining the naked body underneath. Which was quite ridiculous of course, but it made her blush nevertheless, and she was relieved when he turned again to Hardacre.

'Well,' he said, 'she's got the looks all right. But you and me, we both know as it takes more than that, don't we?'

'Of course,' Hardacre said. 'But I assure you she has far more than that.'

'Maybe. So let's see a bit of action. Fred, give us a tinkle on the ivories.'

The other man glanced at Hardacre. 'What you want. A waltz?'

'A waltz will do,' Hardacre said.

The thin man went down into the orchestra pit and started playing a piano. Hardacre took Isabella into the dance while Gage looked on. Very soon he called a halt.

'Nice,' he said. 'Very nice. But it'll take more than a bit of ballroom dancing, you know.'

'Of course,' Hardacre said. 'But we can work up an act. There's talent here.'

'Maybe there is and maybe there ain't. Remains to be seen.' He turned his gaze on the girl. 'Legs.'

She glanced at Hardacre, questioning.

'He wants to see your legs,' Hardacre explained. 'Lift your skirt.'

Somewhat reluctantly she stooped, took hold of the hem of her skirt and raised it slightly.

'Higher,' Gage said. 'Don't be shy, girlie. You wanta be on the stage you gotta forget all that.'

She looked again at Hardacre and he gave her an encouraging smile and said: 'It's all right.'

She gave a shrug, bent down again, grasped the skirt with both hands and pulled it up with the petticoat beneath to the level of her thighs.

'Nice,' Gage said. 'Very nice indeed. Nothing to be ashamed of there, young lady. As fine a pair of pins as ever I see.'

Before they left Hardacre told Isabella to wait in the wings while he had a little talk with Gage. The little talk lasted for at least a quarter of an hour and she was rather tired of waiting when he rejoined her. He looked quite pleased with himself, so she concluded that the little talk had been satisfactory. But all he said was:

'Sorry to have kept you waiting. Now we'll be on our way.'

It was not until they reached home that he said anything at all about the outcome of the talk with Gage, though he must have known she was dying to be told. Even then he said nothing but just hummed a little tune. She could see that he was teasing her, so finally she lost patience and cried:

'Well? How did it go?'

'How did what go, my dear?'

'You know what. Your talk with that man.'

'Gage? Oh, pretty well, pretty well.'

'And what does that mean?'

'It means that he likes the look of you and if we can work up a good dance routine we might just find ourselves taken on. The fact is he's looking for some new blood and we may have come just at the right time. What did you think of him?'

'Well,' she said. And then she stopped, hardly knowing what to say.

Hardacre laughed. 'Bit of a rough diamond, eh? Used to be a stand-up comic at one time.'

'Stand-up comic?'

'A man who gets up on the stage, usually in funny clothes, and tells jokes, often involving his fictitious mother-in-law. Maybe he'll do a little dance and end up with a song. It can be a killer. If the audience don't like you they give you the bird.'

She looked puzzled. 'The bird?'

'That's stage slang. It means you get hissed. If they really dislike you they may start throwing things such as over-ripe tomatoes, rotten fruit, even bad eggs.'

'Did they ever do that to him?'

'I wouldn't be surprised. Anyway, he decided that the management side was more desirable. Let somebody else get up there on the stage and take the knocks.'

He must have noticed a slightly worried expression on her face and he hastened to reassure her. 'Don't let it bother you. They won't throw anything when you're up there, except maybe a bouquet. They'll love you. Take my word for it. You'll have them eating out of your hand.'

She wondered whether he himself had ever experienced that kind of thing. She still knew so little about him. Could it have been a lack of success on the boards that had persuaded him to take the post of dancing-master at Miss Lowther's establishment? Perhaps she had taken him on as a special favour and had been ill repaid for her generosity.

She cast the thought from her mind. In this world you had to look out for yourself, didn't you?

'That man—' she said.

'Walter Gage?'

'Yes. Why did he call you Mr Haitch?'

Hardacre laughed. 'He's a cockney. Born within the sound of Bow Bells. What he meant was Mr H. First letter of my name. As he might call you Miss F.'

'Oh, I see.'

'I think fate may be favouring us. He's aiming to put some new acts in his programme and we may have come along at just the right time.'

She hoped he was right, because if he was not what did the future hold for them? They had both burnt their bridges and could not go back.

He saw her expression and gave a laugh. 'Don't worry, dear girl. We're going to be winners. See if we aren't. Walter Gage is our gateway to success.'

It seemed to her a curious gateway, but she had to believe him.

10

DRESS REHEARSAL

They went to the theatre every morning and worked on the routine. She enjoyed it, for dancing was in her blood. The skinny man named Fred played the piano and Walter Gage watched and made suggestions. They worked at it for a week and they went to a theatrical outfitters and bought costumes.

Isabella wondered where Hardacre was finding the money to buy the gear, and she came to the conclusion that Walter Gage was financing him. It would be an advance on their wages and he would be repaid by their services.

'Walter is taking a gamble on us,' Hardacre said. 'Though really it's not much of a risk. He's a shrewd judge of an act and he can see he's backing a winner in you and me.'

She hoped he was right, but she was nervous and perhaps just a little bit scared. Suppose the audience did not like them. Suppose they were given the bird.

Hardacre told her not to worry about that. He was confident that all would be well.

'They'll love us. Especially you.'

He told her that Gage was getting an entirely new set of acts together. He also told her that it was not really a theatre; it was a music hall.

'They never put plays on in this kind of place, and I doubt whether the audience would appreciate it if they did. It's all variety, a succession of acts. Nobody's on the stage for long.'

She began to meet some of the other performers when rehearsals began. She was sharing a dressing-room with some other girls; only the favoured few had rooms to themselves; you had to earn the privilege.

A young and attractive woman sitting next to her introduced herself as Laura Peart and added the information that she was the conjuror's assistant. In the act she wore tights which showed off her long slim legs to perfection. Gerald Hardacre said all conjurors' assistants were like that because it took the audience's attention off what the man was doing. Isabella doubted this, since it would be only the male section of the audience that was distracted in this way. She thought that for someone who regularly got sawn in half, had swords thrust through her while enclosed in a sealed box and suffered other indignities on stage Miss Peart looked remarkably well.

'Who are you with, dear?' she asked.

Isabella told her, and she looked surprised.

'So what happened to Rita?'

'Rita?'

'Oh, dear!' Miss Peart said. 'Have I said the wrong thing? Forget it, love.'

That evening when they were having supper Isabella repeated the question that Laura Peart had declined to answer.

'Who's Rita?'

Hardacre looked startled and somewhat annoyed. The question had obviously taken him off guard.

'Who told you about her?'

'Miss Peart.'

'Oh, did she? Well, I suppose someone was bound to. So what exactly did she tell you?'

'Nothing really. She just asked what happened to her. And when she realised I knew nothing she shut up.'

'Well, I suppose you may as well know. Somebody's bound to make it their business to tell you eventually. Stage people are no different from anyone else in that respect; they like a bit of gossip, especially if it puts somebody else in a poor light. So the fact is this; Rita Ling used to be my partner. Then she walked out on me and that killed the act.'

'I see,' Isabella said. And it occurred to her that this might have been why he had taken the job of instructing young ladies at Miss Lowther's establishment in the art of dancing. Perhaps it had been his lifeline. And then he had thrown it away for the chance he had seen of resurrecting the act with a new partner. Suppose he had failed. Suppose Walter Gage had turned him down. It hardly bore thinking about.

'Why did she do that?'

'Because a rich swine came along and offered her the chance of leading a life of ease and comfort without having to dance her legs off to keep the wolf from the door. If she's really smart she'll get the wedding ring on her finger before she loses her looks and he gets tired of her.'

He sounded bitter. And perhaps he had reason to be, since it appeared that the defection of Miss Ling had put him out of work, for a dancing partnership is no longer viable when one of the partners decides to call it a day. So when he got himself employed by Miss Lowther he had been on the lookout for a new partner to give his stage career a fresh start. And there he had recognised in her the very one who might fill the bill.

It had been a risk. He had seen her dancing only in the innocent manner that was expected of Miss Lowther's pupils. This was no proof that she could make the leap from drawing-room to stage. It might all have ended in failure. And of course it still might, for the proof could only come when the two of them performed before a critical audience which had no vested interest in their success.

'Were you and Rita a good partnership?' she asked.

He grinned at her. 'Not nearly as good as you and I will be.'

The trouble was that she could not be sure he was not saying this merely to encourage her.

In consultation with Walter Gage they had decided to call themselves Gerald and Bella.

'Could have been Pedro and Carmen,' Gage said. 'Just to give it the Spanish touch. But why bother? It's the performance as counts.'

So on the handbills they became 'Gerald and Bella. Dance of Delight.'

There was an act called Winthrop and Charlie. Winthrop was the comedian and Charlie was the straight man, or what Hardacre called the feed. He fed the material to Winthrop for him to make the laughs.

Winthrop was a tubby man with a rubbery face which he could contort into all manner of grotesque shapes.

'People think he's the clever one because he makes them laugh. But he's not, you know.' Hardacre said.

'No?' Isabella said.

'No. It's Charlie who writes the stuff. Winthrop just puts it across. And Charlie's the nice one. Everybody likes him but they hate Winthrop. He's vain and boastful and he treats Charlie like dirt.'

'So why does he stick with him?'

'That's what everybody wonders. Perhaps because he

knows Winthrop can put the stuff across and he might not find anyone else who could.'

There was an act called 'Professor van Osler and his Performing Dogs'.

'Professor indeed!' Hardacre said. 'People think maybe he's Dutch, and he puts on the accent to fool them. But the fact is he comes from Bootle and his real name is Dredge.'

Hardacre hated animal acts, especially dogs. 'Samuel Johnson had it about right, though he was talking about women parsons. "A woman's preaching", he said, "is like a dog's walking on its hind legs. It is not done well and the wonder is that it is done at all." Or something like that. Damn brutes make a mess in the dressing-room. Need to be fumigated after they been in it.'

Isabella suspected that he was exaggerating. It was just that he disliked dogs. She herself thought they were sweet. She hoped that Gerald would not alienate a fellow performer by being rude to him. But she soon discovered that she need have no fears on this point when she saw him slap Dredge on the back and address him as Professor in the friendliest of manners.

When she taxed him with this he laughed and told her it was advisable never to make enemies in show business because you never knew when they might be in a position to injure you.

'Keep on good terms with everybody, that's the best policy, even if you can't bear the sight of them.'

*

She was nervous when they first rehearsed with an orchestra, but it was really much better than just the piano. She was even more nervous when they came to the dress rehearsal. They were dressed as gypsies tended to be on stage and probably never were in real life. Hardacre had a red and white spotted handkerchief on his head and a voluminous white shirt open at the neck with floppy sleeves buttoned at the wrist. The trousers were black, narrow in the leg and flared at the ankle. All the way down each outer seam was a row of pearly buttons ending at the highly polished black shoes. Brass rings dangling from his ears gave him quite a piratical look.

Isabella, the gypsy maiden, had the feminine equivalent: a pleated blouse and a black skirt that reached down to a few inches below her knees and was wide enough to provide a view of her legs to the top of her thighs whenever she whirled around in the course of the dance. Her hair was swept back from her forehead and tied in a pony-tail with a red ribbon. On one side of her head was an artificial red rose and her earrings matched the bangles on her wrists.

The sight of her might well have been enough to make any young man dream of giving up life in the smoke of the city and going off to live in a caravan and spend his evenings by a campfire.

The dress rehearsal did not go particularly well. Her

nervousness did not help, and when the rose fell out of her hair and she trampled it underfoot this made things worse. She almost stopped then, but Hardacre hissed at her to keep going and somehow she got through the routine without further mishap.

Not all the other acts were free from hitches either, and there were some harsh words handed out. But Gerald told her this was quite normal and not to let it bother her.

'There's a saying: "Bad dress rehearsal, good first night". Things will be fine tomorrow. You'll see.'

She had doubts about that, but she did not say so.

11

DEBUT

The day which was to see the first performance of the pair of dancers calling themselves Gerald and Bella could hardly have been more depressing. It was cold, wet and windy. The wind came in gusts, flinging the rain into the faces of those unfortunate pedestrians who were heading into it. The streets of London were slimy and stank of wet horse droppings. There were umbrellas everywhere, some of them blown inside out by the gusting wind.

Isabella wondered whether people would be kept away from the music hall by the inclement weather. Hardacre said it might, and if the seats were not all filled it would be a poor start to their stage career. It was unusual for him to take such a gloomy view of things and it did nothing to suppress the nervousness she was feeling as the hour of their debut approached.

He must have realised this and hastened to reassure her.

'It'll be all right, though. Even if the house isn't quite full there's bound to be enough to make a go of things. And they're going to like you. I'd stake my life on that.'

She hoped he was right, but still she could not help being nervous. Suppose all did not go well. Suppose she made a hash of things. Suppose they got the bird.

At midday it was still raining, but the wind had dropped. And early in the afternoon the rain ceased. There was still no hint of the sun, but at least they would be able to get to the music hall without being soaked.

'It's a good omen,' Hardacre said. His spirits had obviously risen with the improvement in the weather. 'I take it as an omen that we shall be a great success. Tomorrow everybody will be singing our praises.' He gave a laugh. 'We'll put Professor van Osler and his canine academy in the shade, see if we don't.'

When they got to the music hall Isabella was already feeling quite sick with apprehension. In the dressing-room Miss Peart, the conjuror's assistant, was kind enough to give her encouragement.

'This is your first time before an audience, isn't it, dear?'

Isabella admitted that it was.

'And you'll be nervous, I dare say.'

Isabella did not deny that she was.

Miss Peart put a hand on her arm. 'No need to be. I've watched your act from the wings and you're good. No doubt about it. They'll love you.'

'That's what Gerald says.'

'And he's right. You're better than that Rita ever was. Not that she wasn't good. She was. But there's a difference between just good and top-notch.'

'You think that's what I am?'

'No doubt about it, dearie.'

Isabella had a feeling that the other girl was, in a good-natured way, just trying to encourage her. Which was nice of her and was perhaps more than could have been expected.

But she was nervous nevertheless.

Her mouth was dry and her hands were shaking as she waited with Gerald in the wings, listening to the applause for the preceding act.

'If only,' she thought, 'it was the end of our act and the applause was for us.'

But there was no sense in having thoughts like that, and a little later they were on the stage in the glare of the foot-lights and the curtain was up.

She had caught a glimpse of the first few rows of the audience as they skipped on hand-in-hand and knew that hundreds of eyes were watching them. But she did not think of them because she and Gerald were in the dance and her nervousness had gone. She was dancing her heart out and not giving a thought to those people watching. It was as if she were being swept away out of this world into a dreamland where there was nothing but the sound of the music and the tapping of their feet.

As they took their bow the applause almost drowned the sound of Gerald's voice in her ear: 'I told you so. They love you.'

There were shouts that sounded to her like 'Core! Core!'

'They want an encore,' Gerald said. 'They haven't had enough of us.'

So they danced the rehearsed encore as the orchestra struck up again. Then there was more applause until finally they got off the stage for the last time after taking a curtain call.

She remembered it always. There were even better nights later, but this was the one that stayed in her mind because it was the first and there could never be another quite like it.

There was a backstage celebration after the show. The whole company was there, including Professor van Osler's dogs, each with a bone to gnaw. There had been a full house despite the weather and Walter Gage was pleased. Even Fred looked less gloomy than usual with a glass of milk stout in one hand and a ham sandwich in the other.

Laura Peart, the conjuror's assistant, said she was so pleased it all went well for Isabella.

'But I knew it would. You've got it in you. Wish I had your

talent. All I'm good for is to show my legs and hand things to The Great Martello, as he calls himself.'

'Did you ever try dancing?'

'Oh, I tried. I wasn't all that bad, but I never really made the grade. It has to be born in you, I suppose. Anyway, not to grumble. Mine's a nice steady job and it doesn't tax the brain.'

Isabella liked Miss Peart. She was entirely without guile. With her there was none of the backbiting that some others in the profession were apt to indulge in.

Hardacre said it was because she was too simple-minded. 'If she was more intelligent she'd be doing something more rewarding than acting as assistant to a third-rate magician.'

She wondered why he called The Great Martello third-rate. To her he seemed very good, and she still could not see how the tricks were done. No doubt Laura could have told her why the swords thrust through the box in which she was contained drew no blood, though it should have been streaming out in floods. But it would have been as much as her job was worth to reveal any secrets of The Great Martello's trade.

'It's all done by mirrors,' Hardacre said.

Which was complete nonsense, of course. It just meant that he had no more idea than she had regarding the mechanics of the conjuror's art.

*

She was not so nervous on the second night, and the reception was not quite as rapturous. She wondered why this was. As far as she could tell they were performing just as well as on the opening night.

Gerald told her not to let it bother her. 'It's one of the mysteries of the stage. Take a comedy for instance. One night they're laughing their heads off and the next night there's scarcely a giggle. The night after that it's different again. In this business you have to take the rough with the smooth and just hope they don't start throwing things.'

Well, they were not doing that and she just hoped they never would, because that would be just too awful for words. But she didn't think it was at all likely. Not with their act. Gerald and Bella were good; everyone said so. She felt that she had the world at her feet.

The fact was that though the man was certainly a first rate performer, it was the girl who caught the eye. There was magic in her, every movement she made a delight to watch. He, with the eye of an expert, had probably detected it from the outset and had singled her out to replace the errant Rita.

Sometimes she wondered whether her family knew that she was performing on the stage and earning a living from dancing. She had told her father that this was what she intended doing, but she doubted whether he had believed that it would ever be anything more than a dream.

But just suppose they did find out and decided to come

and see her perform. Suppose she were to take them back-stage and introduce them to people like Winthrop and Charlie, Professor van Osler, The Great Martello and the rest of the performers. What an experience it would be for them.

Now that the nervousness she had felt at first had almost entirely disappeared she found that she enjoyed appearing before an audience. It excited her, gave her a sense of achievement, even of power over all these people.

'Any regrets?' Hardacre asked.

'None at all.'

'Never feel you made a mistake throwing in your lot with me?'

'Oh, no.'

If she had not taken that step she might never have stepped on to the boards of a stage, might never have known the feeling of exhilaration that a wildly applauding audience could arouse.

'I love you, Bella,' he said.

'I love you too.'

But did she? She liked him certainly. She enjoyed being in bed with him. But she had had no experience to tell her what it was like to be really head-over-heels in love with a man. She had had her dreams of course, but in them the Prince Charming had been young and handsome. Gerald was good-looking; that could not be denied; and he had charm of a mature kind. But could a girl as young as she was, truly be in love with a man of his age? Which of course brought up the question of what age he really was. He had never told her and she would not have presumed to ask.

But did it matter anyway? Surely what was really important was that their act should be a success on stage. And of that there could be no possible doubt. The evidence was there each night in the reaction of the audience. Everything was going better than she could ever have hoped for; so why should she bother her head with questions to which she could give no answer?

'You're frowning,' Gerald said. 'Is anything worrying you?'

'Worrying me? No, nothing at all. Everything is going fine, isn't it?'

'It certainly is. We've fallen on our feet, you and I. Fallen on our feet.'

She laughed. He could hardly have chosen a more apt expression.

12

MONSIEUR DUPIN

A year passed. The dance partnership, Gerald and Bella, became well known in the business. They had gained more prominence on the handbills. They had also added singing to the act. Hardacre had a rather fine baritone voice and Isabella was a soprano. They blended very well and, as Hardacre said, it was another string to their bow.

'It's an insurance too. One of us could break a leg.'

She was superstitious and thought it was tempting fate to speak of anything as disastrous as that.

They had done some touring; appearing in places like Nottingham, Manchester and Liverpool, staying in lodgings with landladies who catered for that kind of business. They had long since moved out of the rented house, to which Hardacre had originally taken her and had better quarters whenever they were in London.

Isabella had only a hazy idea of how much they were earning, but she guessed it was enough for a comfortable living. She left it to Gerald to take care of the financial side of things, but whenever she requested money for clothes or anything else he never raised any objection and she was content with this arrangement.

She had never been pregnant and had come to the conclusion that she was not meant to be a mother. She was not sorry. A child would have been a handicap in their line of business, especially when they went on tour.

In one of their London seasons they appeared on the same programme as Marie Lloyd who was at the summit of her career at that time. She had made her name with such songs as 'The Boy I Love Sits Up In The Gallery' and 'My Old Man Said Follow The Van'.

Hardacre maintained that she was not so very wonderful and he could never understand what made her so popular; but Isabella put this down to envy on his part. She herself thought Marie Lloyd was a first-rate performer who deserved her success. She had talked to her and had found her a very pleasant person. But she did not tell Gerald this.

It was at this time that a Frenchman named Henri Dupin appeared on the scene. He was a dapper little man, very smartly dressed, black-haired and sharp-featured, with a trim moustache and a Vandyke beard. He had a remarkably fine set of teeth, and when he spoke the whiteness contrasted sharply with the jet-black of his moustache and beard.

It transpired, after he had introduced himself, that he was in London on a mission, and this mission was to find talent in the entertainment line which might be tempted to make the crossing of the English Channel and appear on the stage in Paris. The stage in question was apparently at a theatre called Le Moulin Rouge.

Isabella, who had studied the French language at the educational establishment of Miss Lowther, had no difficulty in translating this as The Red Mill, which seemed an odd sort of name for a theatre or even a music hall, but she did not remark on this.

Apparently Monsieur Dupin, having seen Gerald and Bella on stage had no doubt whatever that this act would be eminently suitable for the Moulin Rouge. He suggested to Hardacre that they might earn rather more in Paris and at worst it would be a new experience for them.

Isabella was amazed and a trifle shocked at the curtness with which Hardacre rejected the suggestion. He said nothing would induce him to leave England where he had been born and bred. He did not even consult his partner. Apparently she was to have no voice in the matter.

Monsieur Dupin looked surprised and possibly a little put out by the vehemence of the rejection. He glanced at Isabella.

'And you, Madame? Would you not wish to see Paris?'

Before she could reply Hardacre broke in: 'It is immate-

rial whether she would or not. The decision is for me to make, and I have made it.'

With that he turned and walked away.

Dupin gave a very Gallic shrug of the shoulders and a faintly regretful grimace.

'Monsieur Hardacre appears to have a strong dislike of my country. I hope you are not of the same persuasion.'

She hastened to assure him that she was not and to beg him not to take offence at Gerald's rather brusque rejection of his offer.

'If it were up to me, I'd be more than happy to go to Paris. It might be fun.'

'But of course you would not do so without Monsieur?'

'No. That would be quite impossible. We are a pair.'

'Naturally. But if there should ever come a time when you are no longer a pair?'

'Then things would be quite different of course. But I cannot foresee that happening.'

'No, perhaps not. But' – Monsieur Dupin stroked his beard and looked at her thoughtfully – 'if there should ever come a time when the unexpected were to happen and you were no longer linked with Monsieur Hardacre perhaps you would then consider such a move not entirely out of the question.'

He thrust a hand into an inner pocket of his jacket and pulled out a wallet from which he extracted a small pasteboard card which he held out to her.

'That is my address. If you should ever wish to get in touch with me a letter sent there would find me.'

She hesitated to accept the card. What would Gerald say? But then it occurred to her that there was no reason why he should even know. She felt sure she would never have occasion to write to Henri Dupin, but there could be no harm in taking his card, could there?

So she took it.

After that the dapper little Frenchman smiled, kissed her hand and took his leave.

13

CLIMAX

It was some time later when Isabella learned the true reason why Hardacre had such an aversion to the idea of trying his luck in Paris. It was a little shamefacedly that he told her. Apparently, as a young man he had taken a short sea-trip with some other people in a rowing-boat at Brighton, the oars being plied by a weather-beaten old salt in a knitted jersey.

It was a day when the sea, though not absolutely calm, had no more than a lazy swell to impart an up-and-down movement to the boat. Yet this was enough to have a most unpleasant effect on young Mr Hardacre. In fact, to the heartless amusement of the other holidaymakers in the boat, who were not in the least affected by the gentle motion, he was violently seasick.

The experience was so unpleasant that he had vowed never again to venture out to sea in any kind of vessel, large or small. Since it was impossible to get to France without crossing a treacherous stretch of water called by the English 'The English Channel' and by the French 'La Manche', he saw no possibility of accepting Henri Dupin's offer of employment at Le Moulin Rouge.

'Until they build a bridge over that nasty piece of water or dig a tunnel under it I'm staying in England.'

'But surely,' Isabella said, 'seasickness can't be so terribly bad.'

Gerald gave her a sour look. 'Have you ever been seasick?'

Having never been to sea, she had to admit that she had not.

'Then you can have no idea what it's like. So let me tell you, it's absolutely hellish, and it'll take more than Dupin and his damned Moulin Rouge to get me on the briny again.'

She thought he was exaggerating, but there was no point in arguing about it, so she said no more.

It was not long after this that she began to realise that Gerald was developing a drink problem. At first he took pains to hide it from her, and she was so inexperienced in such matters that she did not understand what was making him less than perfect in his dancing. She hesitated to remark on this; it would have seemed too much like criticism and he would most certainly have resented it.

Eventually, however, she felt compelled to ask him

whether he was feeling quite well. His reaction to this innocent inquiry was quite startling. He almost snarled at her.

'Well, of course I'm well. What the devil do you mean? Do
I look ill?'

'No, but—'

'But what?'

'It's just that sometimes in the dance you seem—'

'Seem? Well, out with it. What do I seem?'

She felt intimidated by his angry reaction to what had
been a perfectly harmless question regarding his health.
He appeared to be taking it almost as an insult. So it was
with some hesitation that she replied.

'It's as if just occasionally you lose something in the
dance.'

'Ah!' he said. 'Now we have it. What you're accusing me
of is being too intoxicated to keep the step. In plain
language that I'm drunk. Is that it?'

She was completely taken aback by this question. It had
never entered her head to suspect that his occasional loss
of touch might be the result of slight intoxication. She had
never had any experience of the effects of drunkenness
even in its mildest form. The Fosters had been practically
teetotal, with just a bottle of port at Christmas, of which
the girls were allowed no more than the merest sip. So this
suggestion of Gerald's that she was accusing him of being
drunk on stage came as a most unpleasant shock.
Moreover, it then occurred to her that the faint odour she

had detected on his breath now and then, and which had rather puzzled her, might have been produced by alcoholic liquor of some sort.

'My God!' Gerald said, as though now that the subject had been broached he were unwilling to let it go. 'It's a fine thing if a man can't swallow a drop or two of brandy without having it thrown in his teeth. It's not a crime, you know.'

She tried to protest that she had not been accusing him of anything. But he was not listening. He went on pouring out his grievances.

'This is one hell of a life. It'd drive a man crazy if he didn't take a drop or two now and then.'

She was surprised to hear this. She had always imagined he enjoyed being an entertainer; that he loved the limelight and the applause which to her were so delightful. Now it seemed that he hated it all; that he could endure the life only with the aid of alcohol. But perhaps he was using that simply as an excuse for his tippling.

Whatever the reason, however, it was doing no good at all to the act of Gerald and Bella.

And it got worse. After this revelation it was as if he no longer felt any need to conceal or put a check on his habit. The result was inevitable: their reputation suffered, and soon they could get only the poorest provincial engagements.

The climax came in, of all places, Aberdeen. The act they

were following at the theatre in the Granite City was a pretty girl playing a concertina. She was good, but it should have been an easy act to follow. As it might have been if the male half of Gerald and Bella had not been absent and she had no idea where he was.

She was distraught, but there was nothing she could do but go on stage and do the best she could to improvise a solo performance. It did not go well. How could it? She knew then what it was like to get the bird. It was humiliating. It was also the end of Gerald and Bella as a partnership.

There had been a time when she might have wept. But the years that had passed since her flight to London with Gerald Hardacre had toughened her, mentally as well as physically. She was twenty-one now and she saw that it was time to cut herself adrift from this man who was no longer anything but a burden to her.

He did not come back to their lodgings that night, but in the morning a policeman arrived to inform her that her partner was in a cell, having been arrested the previous evening for being drunk and disorderly.

She visited him at the police station and informed him bluntly that she never wished to see him again. He was abject; stone cold sober now, he pleaded with her not to abandon him; promised to mend his ways and never touch another drop of liquor if only she would stay with him.

But she was adamant. She could see that if she did not break away from him things would only get worse, and she had no intention of sacrificing her own future for the sake of a drunkard.

He did what she had not done. He wept. The sight of his tears disgusted her. It was scarcely believable now that there had been a time when she had been completely under his influence to such a degree that he had been able to persuade her to run away from home and defy her father when he tried to take her back. But four years made a difference. She had been a girl then; now she was a young woman with a future before her in which there was no place for this man.

She went back to the lodgings, packed her bags, paid the landlady and caught the next train that was going south. She had money, for she had for some time been accumulating a fund from the allowance that Gerald gave her in the expectation that she might have need of it some day.

Now that day had come.

14

DUPIN AGAIN

As soon as she arrived in London she wrote a brief letter to Monsieur Henri Dupin and sent it to the address on the card he had given her.

It was as if the man had been waiting expectantly for just such a letter. Three days later he arrived in London and met her at the hotel where she was staying so that Gerald would not be able to find her when he returned to the house, which had been their rented dwelling in the capital.

Monsieur Dupin was delighted to meet her again. He had, so he said, been waiting with hopes that she would write ever since their previous meeting.

'It has been too long, dear lady, far too long. But no matter. The time has come.'

He did not ask about Gerald Hardacre. She told him briefly that they had split up, but gave no reason why. She left it to him to figure that one out for himself.

It was spring, and Dupin made the suggestion that they should spend a few days in London seeing the sights and so on before leaving for France. He had anyway some little pieces of business, as he put it, to attend to, and she would have to get a British passport.

The few days stretched to a week, and Isabella found the company of Henri Dupin a refreshing change from that of Gerald Hardacre in that period when he had been going so rapidly downhill as an alcoholic. Dupin was polite, charming and all that could have been desired in a male escort. So pleasant were those few days when the two of them enjoyed the diversions of London that she was quite sorry when they came to an end. But of course it had to be.

The crossing from Dover to Calais was made on a day when the Channel was so calm that she doubted whether even Gerald would have been seasick had he been with her. But of course he was not and never would be again. That part of her life was finished; another phase was beginning, and what that might hold for her she could only imagine. She could not avoid being more than a little apprehensive, for she was venturing on a new path just as much as she had been when she had run away from her childhood home.

Monsieur Dupin appeared to guess what was going through her mind, for he said: 'You are not afraid, are you?'

'A little,' she confessed.

He gave a smile. 'It is natural. You cannot tell what the future holds and I can only tell you that I am confident all will be well. You have beauty and you have talent. Such a combination makes success inevitable.'

He put a hand on her arm and gave it a little squeeze, as if to impress upon her the truth of his words, and she tried to be as confident as he apparently was. But still the doubts were there at the back of her mind and it was not easy to dismiss them.

From Calais they took the train to Paris. Dupin bought the tickets, having already paid her fare for the Channel crossing. He appeared to be taking it as natural that he should deal with all expenses, and Isabella was content to let him do so, since her own resources were so limited.

It was evening when they reached Paris and Dupin said it was too late to transact any business that day, so the best thing to do would be to get a room for her at a modest hotel where he would call for her in the morning and take her to the Moulin Rouge.

Having found the modest hotel Dupin suggested that as it was some time since they had had a decent meal she might be agreeable to sharing a meal with him at a nearby restaurant. She was hungry and could see no objection to this. Indeed, she was very glad he had made the suggestion.

It was a small restaurant where the patron was also the chef, but the meal was excellent, and she said so.

Dupin smiled. 'Ah,' he said, 'we do some things better in France, as I think you will agree. And when you have lived here for a while you may find much else to admire. I trust so.'

Before taking leave of her at the hotel to return to his home he agreed to call for her at ten o'clock in the morning.

'Sleep well and do not worry about a thing. Tomorrow you start on a new career and I am certain it will be a successful one.'

15

SETTLING IN

The dapper little Frenchman was waiting in the foyer of the hotel when she went down in the morning. The time was precisely ten o'clock.

'Ah!' he said, 'I see we are both creatures of punctuality. I trust you slept well.'

'Very well, thank you.'

It was not wholly the truth. In fact she had slept fitfully and had dreams in which she tried to dance but her feet would not move because of the lead weights attached to them. People were pointing at her and laughing and she wished to run away but could not. However, she thought it inadvisable to tell Dupin this.

'Good. Very good,' he said. 'Now let us be on our way.'

There was a cab waiting outside. The cabbie opened the door for them and Dupin assisted Isabella to get in before following her. The cabbie closed the door, climbed up to his seat, gave a flick of the reins and they were on their way.

It was not far, through streets that appeared to be as busy and muddy as those in London. The cab came to a halt, Dupin got out and helped the girl to follow. She stepped down on to the pavement and Dupin made a gesture with a sweep of the arm.

'Voilà!'

And there it was, Le Moulin Rouge, the Red Mill.

Once, she supposed, there had been a real windmill on that site, grinding corn for the citizens of Paris. Had it been red in those days? Possibly. And then an expanding city had grown up round it and now it was no longer a mill but a place of entertainment.

'This way,' Dupin said.

He conducted her to the stage door and they went inside. It was not so much unlike an English theatre backstage that she felt a strangeness in her surroundings. She was, after all, a professional. It was with this thought that she reassured herself.

They were greeted by a large, heavily-built woman whose height was enhanced by a small mountain of ginger hair piled on top of her head like the coils of a sleeping serpent. She had a prominent bust which served as support for the strings of gaudy beads which encircled her neck, and her dress was as colourful as an artist's palette.

She greeted them with effusion and, as was natural, in French.

'Ah! You have arrived. I have been waiting for you. And

this is the young lady.' She gave Isabella a keen appraising look as if seeking any defects there might have been in her appearance; and then, apparently having discovered none, gave her verdict. 'Charming. Quite charming.'

'As I told you,' Dupin said.

'As you told me, Monsieur. But beauty is not everything. Has she talent? That is the question.'

'And the answer to that is: most certainly yes, she has. As you will discover.'

Isabella might have been less embarrassed listening to this exchange if she had not been able to understand what was being said. But the fact was that she could. The teaching of French at Miss Lowther's school had been done by a Frenchwoman who was married to an English engineer. Isabella Foster had been her favourite pupil because she had shown such an aptitude for the subject. Dupin had been pleasantly surprised when she had first spoken to him in his own language.

'That,' he said, 'is one handicap removed from your path when you go to France. Had you been able to speak only English it might have made things difficult.'

Isabella gathered that the large lady, whose name was Madame Cochet, was the one whose approval she had to gain. However, she was later to learn that it was Henri Dupin who wielded much of the power. Apparently he was a very wealthy man and had capital invested in a variety of enterprises; the Moulin Rouge being only one of them. It seemed to please him to search around for new talent to put on the stage, and as he was a shrewd judge in such matters he was allowed to have his way.

As things turned out Isabella was to see him only very occasionally in the future. Having discovered her in London and brought her to Paris it was as if he felt that as far as he was concerned the job was done. She was now in the ample hands of Madame Cochet, and as it turned out her future at the Moulin Rouge was assured.

It was arranged that she should have lodgings with a young dancer named Juliette LeBlanc, a slim blonde girl with a doll-like face and a voice that was seldom raised much above a whisper. The lodgings were in the Montmartre district and had formerly been occupied by a young artist who had decided to end a futile struggle for recognition by throwing himself in the Seine.

Miss LeBlanc had formerly shared her two-bedroom apartment with another dancer, but that young lady had fallen for a handsome suitor with plenty of money and had departed with the avowed intention of never setting foot on a stage again.

'Her heart wasn't in it,' Miss LeBlanc said, and sighed.

Isabella was to discover that she did quite a lot of sighing.

As well as the two bedrooms there was a small sitting-room and an even smaller kitchen where they cooked late-night suppers with ingredients bought at a nearby market. Juliette had scarcely ever been out of Paris and was an enchanted listener when Isabella described some of the attractions of London.

She sighed. 'How I should like to go there some day.'

'And why not? Maybe we could go together. I would be your guide.'

The girl clapped her hands with delight. 'Oh, wouldn't that be splendid. Just the two of us.' Then she sighed again. 'But of course it will never happen. It's just a dream.'

Isabella reflected that she might be right at that. She had hardly got to know Miss LeBlanc and here she was suggesting a trip to London. What could be more unlikely?

Now and then she paused to wonder what Gerald was doing now that she had left him. But she had no regrets; life with him had become impossible and she had taken the only course open to her. From this time forward her life was set on a new course and there was no profit in looking back.

16

L'ANGLAISE

It was quite remarkable how quickly she became an integral part of the programme at the Moulin Rouge. It was as though there had been a vacancy simply waiting for her to fill it.

Madame Cochet said she was not surprised for she knew she could rely on the judgement of Monsieur Dupin.

'He is never wrong. It is quite amazing. He has the eye, as one might say, and we are fortunate to benefit from it.'

Isabella could only feel glad that not only did Henri Dupin have the eye but that this eye should have discovered her. For there could be no doubt that, if she was good for the Moulin Rouge, the Moulin Rouge was certainly good for her. She had both figuratively and literally fallen on her feet, and those feet were her fortune.

Soon she was a favourite with audiences. She became known as L'Anglaise, adored by the clientèle and liked by her fellow artistes for her complete lack of pretension. She knew that as an alien she might be regarded by the other performers as something of an intruder, so for her own sake she decided to tread warily, even though she could detect no evidence of anglophobia in any of those with whom she worked.

She asked Juliette LeBlanc whether she had heard any nasty remarks made about her behind her back because she was English.

Miss LeBlanc seemed astonished that she should suspect any such thing.

'Why should anyone do that? Everybody loves you.'

Isabella suspected that this was perhaps an overstatement from an observer who might be more than a little biased; but it could have been close enough to the truth if you substituted 'like' for 'love'.

'You really are a sweet girl, Juliette,' she said, and was surprised to see the sweet girl go quite pink in the face.

She had not been working at the Moulin Rouge long before making the acquaintance of a man who had such short legs that he was little taller than a dwarf. The girls all seemed to be on good terms with him and addressed him as Toulouse, which seemed odd to her, since Toulouse was surely a town in the south of France. Then she heard that his name was Toulouse-Lautrec, that he came from an upper class family and was regarded by them with some disapproval because of the dissolute kind of life he led and the low company he kept.

She also learned that the reason why his legs were so short was that as a child he had fallen off a horse and damaged them so badly that they had ceased to grow any longer. As a result he was condemned to go through life when he grew older with a man's body mounted on a boy's legs. How much truth there was in this explanation, which sounded rather unlikely to her, it was impossible to say. But certain it was that his torso and shoulders were bulky enough, as well as his head with its black hair and prominent nose supporting a pair of spectacles through which he possibly took a rather jaundiced view of a life that had made him something of a freak.

That he was a gifted freak there could be no doubt. He was an artist and painted pictures of the Moulin Rouge performers for posters advertising the show. He painted one of Isabella, but she was not greatly pleased with it. She thought it was more of a caricature than a portrait. It was certainly not flattering.

What was perhaps more flattering was the artist's attempt to seduce her. She could not imagine making love with such a grotesque. She told Juliette about this experience and was informed that it was not by any means unique.

'He has something of a reputation in that respect.'

'You mean he has tried it with others?'

'Yes. And with some success.' She gave a giggle. 'I've heard that he is quite a remarkable lover.'

Isabella stared at her. 'You have heard?'

Miss LeBlanc smiled. 'Oh, I do not speak from experience. I don't think he has ever been attracted to me. I am one of those he has not painted.'

Isabella thought this might have been because the other girl was no great beauty, though she was far from plain. The blonde hair was almost golden in colour and her eyes were a deep blue, the nose small and retroussé and the lips slightly pouting. She was good-natured and one might have had a far less pleasant colleague with whom to share one's lodgings.

Then one night, six months since she had moved in, another side to Miss LeBlanc's character was revealed to Isabella.

She was not sure how long she had been asleep but she woke to find that she was not alone in her bed. Someone else had crept in beside her, and this someone was caressing her. It took her no more than a moment to realise that it had to be Juliette and her immediate reaction was one of shock and an instinctive movement away from the caressing hand. But there was little room in the bed for any such movement and the realisation came to her that she rather enjoyed the caresses, the fingers that were moving gently over her body.

She said nothing, and the other girl said nothing either. After a while she dropped off to sleep again.

When she woke in the morning she was alone in the bed

and she began to wonder whether it had been nothing but a dream.

At breakfast neither of them said anything regarding what might or might not have occurred in the night. They spoke of other things and Isabella came to the conclusion that she must after all have dreamed that she had had a visitor to her bed and that the incident had never occurred in fact.

Which would have been a perfectly believable conclusion if the experience had not been repeated the following night. She had scarcely got into bed and blown out the candle when someone came into the room and got in beside her. This was certainly no dream; and though she said nothing, Juliette began fondling her as on the previous night.

Still neither of them said anything, but this time Juliette stayed until morning before leaving. Soon it had become the regular thing for them to sleep together and the fondling was a mutual thing. In the warmer weather they slept naked. Their fingers probed each other's body, and rather to her own surprise Isabella discovered that there was much enjoyment in this.

Things went on in this way for almost a year. And they might well have continued if something had not occurred to bring this happy state of affairs to an abrupt conclusion.

Isabella fell in love.

And not with Juliette.

17

OTTO

Otto Axter-Mandel was a German, and since it was only a few years since a German army had been besieging Paris it might have been expected that he would not have been at all popular at the Moulin Rouge. But Otto had two great advantages: he was young and he was very very rich. He was also handsome and spoke perfect French with only the merest suggestion of a German accent.

Moreover, the Germans, although they had caused some discomfort to the besieged Parisians, had never actually entered the city. It was true that the French and the Germans had been historically opposed to one another on the field of battle, but those Germans had usually been Prussians and Otto was not a Prussian, he was a Bavarian. Also he was a well-mannered young man and his possession of considerable wealth was common knowledge.

He had an elder brother, Carl, who was a count and had

a vast estate which would be handed down to Otto if his brother died first, since Carl was unmarried and had no son to inherit the title and land.

Taking all this into account, it was hardly surprising that Otto should be made welcome at the Moulin Rouge and that he should be taken backstage when he made a request to meet some of the performers. Moreover, when he said some of the performers it turned out that in fact, he meant one of them in particular: Isabella Foster, known as L'Anglaise.

It was thus that Otto Axter-Mandel met Isabella Foster, and if it was not for both of them love at first sight it was certainly something very close to it. And this was hardly remarkable, since Isabella was undoubtedly very beautiful and Otto was a handsome young man, six feet tall, well-built, with fair hair and sea-blue eyes. He also had delightful manners. What more could any woman demand?

He took her out to lunch the next day at a fashionable restaurant and described in glowing terms the estate to which he would shortly return. When he took her out to lunch a second time he asked her to go with him. He also told her that he loved her, that he was mad about her and would be devastated if she refused.

Had she been more sophisticated she might not have accepted the invitation as readily as she did. She might have pretended not to believe he was serious. She might also have said that it was quite impossible, that she could not leave the Moulin Rouge where she was engaged as a performer.

She said none of these things.

She said: 'I shall have to break my contract.'

'And that bothers you?'

'A little.'

'But you will do it?'

'Yes.'

Madame Cochet was not pleased.

'You are going away just like that?'

'I am sorry.'

'Don't you think you are being a trifle foolish?'

'Perhaps.'

'But it makes no difference?'

'No.'

'You imagine, of course, that you are in love with this man?'

'I know I am.'

'After so short a time? What is it? Two days? Three?'

'Time makes no difference.'

'On the contrary. It makes all the difference in the world. As you will see, I fear. And of course he is in love with you?'

'I believe so.'

'He has told you he is, no doubt.'

'Yes.'

'Phoey!' Madame Cochet gave a snap of the fingers. 'Men

will say anything, promise anything, to serve their own ends. So off you go to this estate somewhere in Germany and maybe for a time all is well. Two turtledoves. Then he tires of you. Maybe you tire of him. And what then? You come back to Paris expecting to have your old job back. But somebody else has taken it. What then?'

'It will not be like that,' Isabella said.

But she knew that it could be. She knew that Madame Cochet was telling the truth. Madame was a woman with experience and knew the way of the world.

Isabella felt a twinge of conscience. This woman had been very good to her, and now it was as if she were letting her down by quitting the Moulin Rouge just when she had become a favourite with the patrons. Nevertheless, she had no intention of changing her mind.

'You don't imagine, I suppose, that he will marry you?'

Isabella was silent. Neither she nor Otto had made any mention of the possibility of marriage. She doubted whether the thought had even entered his mind. In her mind it had been no more than a passing thought; something perhaps to be brought up later, but certainly not imminent.

'No, of course not,' Madame Cochet said. 'He is a nobleman even if he is a German. He would not be expected to marry a dancer from a Paris theatre. When he does marry, as I have no doubt he will in the course of time, it will be to one of his own kind, not an entertainer from the Moulin Rouge, popular as she may be.'

All of which Isabella had to admit to herself was probably true. But it made no difference to the decision she had made. Come what may in the unforeseeable future, she was not going to change her mind.

Madame Cochet accepted the fact and gave a shrug of her shoulders.

'Very well then. So be it. And in spite of everything I wish you well. I sincerely hope that you will never come to regret taking this step.'

And then Madame Cochet did a most remarkable thing; she flung her arms round Isabella and hugged her to her ample bosom. There was even a hint when she released her of a tear or two in her eye. But this might have been merely imagined by the younger woman, since her own vision was certainly rather blurred at the time.

There could be no doubt regarding the tears in Juliette LeBlanc's eyes when the news was broken to her. She wept unashamedly.

'You are leaving Paris? You are going to Germany with that man?'

'Yes.'

'And I shall never see you again?'

'But of course you will,' Isabella assured her. 'There will be visits to Paris.'

'With him?'

'Well, yes.'

'So it will not be the same. Never again.'

Which was true, of course. And could she be sure there would be any visits? All would depend on Otto. Perhaps he had had his fill of Paris and would have no desire to see the place again.

'Have you not been happy living with me?'

'Very happy.'

'Then why—?'

'Because—' But how could one explain the inexplicable? 'Because I have to. Don't cry. Soon you will forget me.'

'Never.'

'Ah, you think so now. But time changes everything.'

And that, she thought, was a platitude which gave no consolation.

'I will write to you,' she said.

And knew it was a lie.

18

CARL

They travelled the first part of the way by train. It was a two-day journey and the final part was made by coach. It was dark when they arrived but there were lights burning in the schloss and some outside, so that Isabella gained an impression of the great size of the place.

Otto had already explained to her that, though of course it all belonged to his brother Carl, the Count, as a bachelor, had no need of the whole building and allowed Otto to occupy one wing where he could do as he wished without bothering the older man.

'You will meet him of course, but not tonight. He goes to bed early.'

The coach had stopped on a broad forecourt and there were wide steps leading up to the front door. Servants had come to take their luggage and Otto gave orders in German which she could not understand. It brought home to her the fact that she was now in a foreign land. She had become so used to living in Paris and speaking French that she had come almost to regard France as her native country. She saw that it would be necessary now to learn a third language. Perhaps Otto would teach her. It might be fun.

They went through a wide doorway into a vast tiled entrance hall from which other doors opened from left and right and two staircases ascended to a balcony.

'Come,' Otto said. 'I will show which is my part of the house.'

They had supper in a dining-room in which the polished mahogany table would have accommodated a banquet for forty. Places had been set for them at opposite ends of the table, but Otto said this was ridiculous. They would have had to shout at each other to carry on a conversation. So they both sat at one end and were waited on by a butler and two assistants.

'Tomorrow,' Otto said, 'I will show you round the place and I hope you'll like it.'

'I'm sure I'll love it.'

'Well, we shall see. You will also meet my brother.'

This, if the truth were told, rather scared her. Suppose the Count took a dislike to her. Suppose he disapproved of Otto's conduct in bringing her there. In her imagination Carl appeared as something of an ogre.

They retired to bed soon after supper. She was conducted to her bedroom by a young maidservant who was plain but smiled a lot and said very little; which was just as well, since whatever she did say was unintelligible to Isabella.

The bedroom was larger than any she had ever slept in. Someone had already unpacked her luggage and she felt somewhat ashamed of the scantiness of the clothing that was almost lost in the vast wardrobe which could easily have accommodated twenty times the amount.

The bed was commodious in proportion, and when she got in she felt engulfed in sheets which had been pleasantly heated by a warming-pan which the maid had brought with her.

She snuggled down and tried to sleep, but sleep was elusive. So much was running through her mind to keep her awake. And then, when she had almost dosed off, she was brought back to complete wakefulness by someone slipping into the bed beside her.

'Otto!'

She heard him laugh. 'Who else?'

She felt his hands on her, the fingers caressing, searching. There was no more sleep after that; not for quite a while. It was her first night at the schloss and it was to be a memorable one.

The meeting with Carl, which she had been secretly dreading, took place late the next morning in his part of the building. It was the library, a room in which the walls were lined with shelves of books; so many, she thought, that it would have taken anyone a lifetime to read. To get to this room they had to pass through a long gallery where portraits of the family ancestors, both male and female, hung in gilded frames, most of which had become tarnished with the passage of time. A few of the men were in armour, and all, both men and women, exhibited the changing of fashion over the years and even centuries.

Otto dismissed them all with a flip of the hand and a mocking laugh. 'All dead and gone. A horrible lot, don't you think?'

She said nothing. She was not sure whether or not he was joking. Perhaps he was really rather proud of his distinguished ancestors. Some of the women in ruffs bore an odd resemblance, she thought, to pictures she had seen of Queen Elizabeth.

When they entered the library they discovered the elder brother sitting at a desk with a pen in his hand. He dropped the pen at once, pushed back his chair and stood up. There was a considerable gap of years between the two brothers and there was little resemblance in their features. It made her think that perhaps they had had different mothers. All she had been told by Otto was that the parents were dead, leaving Carl with the title and the estate.

He was a tall, rather stooping man with craggy features and sparse hair beginning to turn grey.

He began to speak in German, then stopped abruptly and started again in rather guttural French.

Suddenly she realised that he was as shy of her as she was of him. He was no master of the French language, as Otto was, but she gathered that what he was trying to say was that he was very pleased to meet her and he hoped that her stay at the schloss would be an enjoyable one.

She replied that she was sure it would be, and after that they very soon left him to carry on with whatever it was he was doing before they interrupted him.

'Some day,' Otto said, 'you must get him to show you his collections.'

'So he is a collector. And what does he collect?'

'Almost anything. You'll see. I'm sure he'll be delighted to show you. Not many people are interested.'

'Does that include you?'

Otto grinned. 'It's not really in my line. I think he's given up on me. As you may have noticed, Carl and I are not exactly twins, in looks or tastes. We get on very well with each other largely because we are so seldom together. You saw all those books in the library? I wouldn't be surprised if he's read every one of them.'

'And you?'

Again he grinned. 'Do I look like a bookworm?'

She was not sure what a bookworm looked like, or even if they had any distinguishing features, but she felt quite certain he was not one. It occurred to her that she could not remember when she herself had last had a book in her hands. Yet as a child she had loved reading. So why had she allowed such a pleasure to vanish from her life?

She was still turning this question over in her mind when Otto said: 'Come. Let's go outside.'

19

COLLECTIONS

Viewed in daylight from the outside the schloss reminded Isabella of one of the more magnificent English country mansions that she had seen in pictures. It was built on a gentle slope so that from the front entrance one descended by wide steps to the shingled forecourt. In the centre of this was a fountain in the form of a nymph holding in her hands a ewer from which a constant flow of water descended to the pool in which she stood.

Beyond the fountain she could see a great park on which deer were grazing. In the distance a lake was visible, glinting in the sunlight. There were clumps of trees here and there and the total effect was wholly pleasing to the eye.

'It's beautiful,' Isabella said.

Otto answered, as though this were an idea that had never occurred to him until she mentioned it: 'Yes, I suppose it is.'

'How far does it extend?'

'Quite a way. We must go riding to take a look.'

'But I don't ride. I have never been on a horse.'

'Then I must teach you. And on the lake we can go sailing. That I will teach you also. There is so much to do here. One need never be bored.'

'Oh,' she said, 'I am sure of that.'

For how could one be bored with Otto for a companion? And a lover.

He took her to look at the garden, which was immense. It was the kind that could only have been maintained by a small army of gardeners. Not for the first time she wondered just how rich the Axter-Mandels were and how they had come by their wealth. Perhaps ancestors had acquired it in the past by pillage or other dubious means and later generations had maintained it by shrewd investment so that now Carl could amuse himself with his hobbies and Otto could live the playboy life with no concern regarding the expense.

Anyway, it was no concern of hers. For her love was everything and she was living in the present with no concern for the future. She refused to contemplate the possibility, even the certainty that this way of life would not go on for ever; indeed, that it might be of only brief duration.

That first day they walked in the garden, inhaled the heady scent of the flowers and sat in the sun.

'Tomorrow,' Otto said, 'your riding lessons begin.'

'I look forward to it,' she said, 'with pleasure.'

For would not any activity in his company be a delight?

The riding lessons began soon after breakfast the next day. Otto picked a docile mare from a number of horses in the stables at the rear of the house. She had no riding-habit but he said this did not matter for the present; she could get one later. A groom fixed a side-saddle and held the bridle while Otto helped her to mount. She found this easy. As a dancer she had a body that was strong and supple. Under Otto's tuition she had by the end of the morning mastered the basic skill of riding.

She had also acquired a sore bottom.

Three days later they rode out to the lake. It was an idyllic spot: limpid water ruffled by a light breeze, shingly beaches here and there, an island in the centre, the rustle of leaves in the trees as they shivered in that same faint movement of air which was affecting the lake.

For a while they just sat on their horses and admired the view.

'What do you think of it?' Otto asked.

'It's wonderful. And all this is part of your estate?'

'All this and much more. Though of course it's not mine; it's Carl's. I'm only the younger brother, you know.'

'And does he come out here?'

'Let's just say it's not a frequent event. Riding a horse is not one of his favourite relaxations. And that's an under-statement. He seems to prefer the four walls of the library to any physical exercise in the open air.'

There was a boathouse on the shore. They tethered the horses and Otto led the way to it. Inside were two boats, one equipped with a mast and sail.

'Would you care for a trip to the island?' he asked.

Isabella was ready to agree to any suggestion on his part, and soon they were in the boat and out of the boathouse. Otto stepped the mast and hoisted the sail. Progress was slow in the light breeze, but they had all the time in the world and were in no hurry. When they reached the island they went ashore and explored that small domain. That done they just lay and basked in the sun and let time go by.

'And this,' she thought, 'is only the beginning.'

Before her in imagination stretched an endless succession of idle sunny days spent in the company of this man she loved to distraction.

Some days they would go for a ride in one of the coaches that were housed near the stables. In the villages people stopped what they were doing to watch them pass. Some of the roads were full of potholes that made the coach shake and rattle. Otto said that in winter the mud became so deep they were practically impassable, especially when it snowed.

The nearest town of any size was Ulm, which could be reached in less than an hour by coach with four horses providing the traction. Whenever they went to town Otto would buy a piece of jewellery such as a diamond brooch or bracelet or necklace for Isabella. It was always an expensive item and he would never look at anything cheaper. Now and then her conscience would prompt her to protest that he was spending far too much on these gifts, but he brushed the suggestion aside.

'It's my pleasure to buy things for you. And besides, no woman can have too much jewellery.'

Much later she was to remember these words and wonder whether even then he was looking to the future when she might have need of such rich gifts. But it certainly did not occur to her at the time.

Occasionally they went to Berlin, but that was a long journey, first by road to Ulm and thence by rail. They would put up at a grand hotel for a week or two and go to the theatre and the opera.

Isabella had never seen an opera and was enchanted by Mozart's 'The Marriage of Figaro', the first that Otto took her to.

'You see now what you have been missing,' he said.

Later they were to see 'Don Giovanni' and Verdi's 'Rigoletto', both of which she loved.

She was rather surprised to find that Otto had this taste for grand opera, but there was much about him that she was to discover in those first few months of their relationship.

One thing that soon became apparent to her was that he had no intention of introducing her to any of the other landowning families with whom he was acquainted. The reason he gave was that they were all very dull and she would be bored to tears if she had to spend an evening with any of them.

It was a lame excuse and she did not accept it.

'I believe you are ashamed of me.'

He laughed at this, though the laughter sounded to her a trifle forced. 'Ashamed of you! Quite the opposite, my dear. If I introduced you to those people all the men would try to seduce you and all the women would hate you for being so much more attractive than they are. I am protecting you from that.'

She still did not believe him, but she let the subject drop.

Once when he had departed in full evening dress for one of these parties that, according to him, she would have found so deadly boring she decided to pay a visit to the elder brother. She did so with some trepidation, not knowing what kind of reception she would receive, yet encouraged by Otto's statement that Carl would be delighted to have someone express an interest in his collections.

So she made the journey through the long picture gallery and came to the door of the library where she hoped to find him. Her first tentative rap on the door produced no result and she thought that perhaps he was not there. However, she tried again with a somewhat louder knock and after a few moments heard shuffling footsteps on the other side of the door before it was opened a little way and Carl peered out.

He appeared surprised to see her, but not, as she had feared, at all annoyed.

'Oh,' he said, 'it's you, Miss Foster.' And then he opened the door wider and invited her to come in.

She did so, and said diffidently: 'I hope I'm not disturbing you.'

'Oh, not at all, not at all. What can I do for you?'

'Otto tells me that you are a collector.'

'That is so.'

'He also said you would be pleased to show me your collections.'

It was remarkable how his craggy features seemed to light up when she said this.

'And you wish to see them?'

'If it is not too much trouble.'

'No trouble at all. I will show you the way.'

It was a room even bigger than the library, and the first things that caught her eye, in the light of the lamp that he had carried from the library, were the big glass-fronted cabinets in which were displayed a great range of stuffed birds. Birds of every size and description were there, from eagles and vultures and a solitary albatross to tiny wrens and robins. All were neatly ticketed with their scientific names as well as their common ones and were perched on twigs or larger branches and even rocks to lend realism to the display.

'It is not complete, I'm afraid,' Carl said. 'But what collection ever is? I continue to search. I have my contacts far and wide.'

He collected butterflies and moths, which she thought were very pretty. The stuffed animals were truly lifelike, including a polar bear standing on its hind legs and apparently about to grab anyone venturing near it with its paws.

There were books of postage stamps which must have come from every country in the world. And then there were the coins displayed on boards with the usual neat little tickets identifying them. She noticed the heads of Caesars on some of them; and these were not the oldest.

So absorbed had she become in all this great collection with the collector himself at her elbow eagerly describing and explaining how he had come by this thing and another, that the hours slipped away uncounted.

She thanked him before leaving. 'It has been so enjoyable.'

It was obvious that he was pleased. 'You must come again. Any time, any time. I am never too busy.'

20

A DEATH IN THE FAMILY

It became a regular practice when Otto was away. She would visit the elder brother and he would show her parts of his collections and tell her the history of this or that object.

She was picking up the German language in that quick way she had with foreign tongues, so that very soon it became almost as easy to converse in German as in the French which he mangled so badly.

He lent her books from the library, some of which were beautifully illustrated. She did not read them but returned them with thanks for the pleasure they had given her.

He said that it was his pleasure to lend them. And she believed him because he was not the kind of man to say things he did not mean.

Otto was amused. 'Be careful. He'll be falling in love with you.'

She told him not to talk nonsense. But to tell the truth

she was not so sure it was nonsense. She remembered how his eyes seemed to light up when he opened the library door and saw who it was that had knocked. And how the colour mounted to his cheeks if their hands chanced to touch in the passing of a book from one to the other. So could there be anything in it? And if there was, what complications might it cause?

Meanwhile, as the months passed, her own love affair with Otto seemed to have entered a new phase. She supposed it was inevitable that that first ecstatic period when it seemed there could be no limit to their passion for each other must come to an end. The flame could not burn so fiercely for ever; that fact had to be faced.

They were, of course, still deeply in love; it would have been a kind of betrayal to doubt it. But it was love of a different order, and the love-making had become a kind of routine, a habit.

So things might have gone on indefinitely had it not been for one shocking event: the murder of Count Carl Axter-Mandel.

It happened one night in early summer and was not discovered until morning. Then a servant came to Otto in great distress to report that the Count had been found in the room where the collections were kept. He was lying on the floor with a knife in his chest and a lot of blood on the body.

Everything pointed to the conclusion that he had surprised a thief in the act, since it could be seen that a window had been forced open and one of the Count's collections of ancient coins was scattered on the floor, apparently dropped by the thief in his haste to get away.

It seemed to Isabella that Otto was more angered than distressed by the crime. It was the audacity of someone daring to break into the schloss and kill his brother that apparently affected him more than the death of that brother.

She herself wept. She and Carl had never been lovers in the sense that she and Otto were, but now that he was gone she realised that she had loved this shy, rather inarticulate man. She realised too that things in that great house would never be the same again; that with this death a vital change had come about which might well mark another turning-point in her life.

It was very easy to catch the murderer. He himself must have realised that it was inevitable, for he made scarcely any attempt to avoid arrest.

They found him in his cottage on the estate with some of the coins he had stolen. He had been one of the outdoor employees until he had been fired for some petty misdemeanour. He had a wife and two young children, a boy and a girl, and no doubt he had been at his wits' end to provide for them now that no wages were coming in. So in desperation he had decided to rob his former employer. He must have heard about the collection of coins that the Count possessed and decided to steal them, although a moment's reflection should have warned him that, even if he succeeded in stealing the coins, he could not have used them to buy as much as a single loaf of bread. They would have had to be sold for what they were: collectors' items. And where could he have hoped to sell them?

It was possible that the act had been seen by him as a form of revenge for his dismissal. But if so, it was ironical that he had killed the wrong man. It was Otto who had dismissed him without even mentioning it to his brother, who would probably have been too soft-hearted to take away his livelihood.

So he was arrested without delay in front of a weeping wife and two small children, who would no doubt be thrown out of their home to make way for a new employee.

'What will happen to them?' Isabella asked.

Otto shrugged. 'That is no concern of mine.'

She thought this was heartless of him, but she said nothing.

'The man of course will be tried. It should not take long. His guilt is obvious.'

'And then?'

'The axe.'

She shivered. How could he speak so coldly of the chopping off of a man's head? To her it seemed a terrible thing.

'Perhaps,' he said, 'you would like to watch the execution. It would be an interesting experience for you. I am told that quite often the headsman, either through lack of skill or nervousness, does his job so clumsily that two or even three cuts are necessary.'

Again she shuddered. 'Nothing would induce me to watch such a horrible spectacle.'

'Ah, you are too squeamish. And after all, the punishment is deserved, is it not?'

He left her then to ruminate on how one fell act had changed the entire situation in the schloss. Things now would never be the same again.

21

MARRIAGE PLANS

'I think it is time for me to get married and have a son,' Otto said.

Isabella said nothing. She waited for him to enlarge upon this statement. And after a while he did so.

'While Carl was alive there seemed to be no urgency, although strictly speaking the situation was no different from what it is now. He was unmarried and childless, so I was the heir presumptive. But there was always the remote possibility that he might marry and produce an heir. Now that possibility no longer exists. I am the Count and if I were to die the title and estate would pass to my cousin, Hermann.'

'Would that be such a bad thing?'

'It would be a disaster. I can think of no one less fit to be my heir. That must be avoided at all cost. Therefore, as I have said, I must marry.'

Isabella was silent. It was apparent that when he spoke of

marriage he was not suggesting that she should be his wife. A dancer from the Moulin Rouge whom he had regarded as being unfit to be introduced to his friends and acquaintances was hardly likely to come into the reckoning as a possible spouse. Nor was it possible that she would be retained as a mistress when a newly wedded wife arrived on the scene. Indeed, she herself would never have accepted that role.

'So,' she said, 'what you are telling me is that I am no longer welcome here. Is that it?'

He gave a shrug. 'It was always inevitable. You yourself must have realised that things could not go on like this indefinitely. It has been good while it lasted, hasn't it?'

'Oh, very good.' She spoke with a trace of bitterness. 'I must have been a fool to imagine it might last. But I did. I suppose you did not.'

He shrugged again, but said nothing.

'When do you wish me to leave?'

'There is no immediate urgency.'

'Perhaps not. But now that the decision has been made I would prefer not to delay my departure.'

'I see that you are being sensible,' he said. 'And of course it is not as if you will be leaving empty-handed.'

She guessed that he was referring to the jewellery. Perhaps in addition he would hand her some money. It was rather degrading. Now that her services were no longer required she was being paid off. But she was far too level-headed to throw the jewels at his feet in a fit of pique or even to refuse any cash that he might hand out. She was still young, but the future was uncertain.

She departed later in the week with more luggage than that with which she had arrived. Otto had indeed given her a generous amount in marks to go with the jewellery, so it could certainly not have been said that she was leaving empty-handed.

He accompanied her to the railway station at Ulm, riding in one of the estate coaches. He bought her ticket and saw her on to the train, wished her luck and kissed her goodbye. But the kiss was so different from those earlier kisses that she remembered. It was perfunctory, a mere peck, meaningless. Everything was so different from that journey from France a year ago. Then she had been eager and excited, with the man she loved beside her. Now the love had faded and she was travelling alone to an uncertain future. Moreover, on this journey she had to fend for herself with no one to see to everything for her.

It was a two-day journey and she arrived in Paris late in the morning, jaded and with a slight headache. She lost no time in converting her German marks into French francs, and then engaged a cab to take her to a hotel where she booked a room. Having left her luggage there, she took her jewels to a bank which she had used during her previous sojourn in the city and deposited all except one ring. This she wore as a reminder of better times.

It was too late now to pay a visit to the Moulin Rouge and she decided to leave it until the next day. She was not at all sure what kind of reception she would get from Madame Cochet when she went there, but she felt confident that Juliette LeBlanc would give her a rapturous welcome. She felt a twinge of conscience for not having carried out her promise to write to her former lodging partner. In fact thoughts of the girl had never entered her head until now; there had been too much else to think about. But now all that was in the past and her great hope was that she might start again where she had left off when she had departed with Otto Axter-Mandel; now Count Otto and lost to her for ever.

22

DARK SECRET

Madame Cochet did not say: 'I told you so', though she might have been tempted to do so. For had not events turned out very much as she had predicted?

What she did say was: 'You're looking very well, my dear. Is this merely a brief visit to Paris or are you here to stay?'

'I am here to stay.'

'Ah! And does that mean you are seeking employment?'

'I shall have to earn a living.'

Madame sighed gustily. 'That, I fear, is a necessity which most of us encounter when there is no one else to foot the bills for us.'

It was the only guarded reference she made to the man Isabella had departed with so many months ago.

Now she said: 'I imagine you will not have kept in practice during your absence.'

Isabella had to admit that she had not.

'So it will take a little time for you to get back into form. You have put on a little weight perhaps?'

'It is possible.'

'It is probable. Where are you staying?'

'In a hotel room for the present. I shall have to find some suitable accommodation.'

'Undoubtedly.'

'I thought perhaps, if no one has taken my place sharing lodgings with Juliette LeBlanc—'

Madame Cochet stared at her. 'You have not heard?'

Isabella sensed immediately that it was something bad she had not heard, and she simply shook her head.

'No, of course not. You have been in another country. The news would hardly have been important enough to cross the border. That poor girl.'

'Juliette?'

'Of course. Who else?'

'Tell me, Madame. What happened?'

'It was just after you left. The very next day. She threw herself into the Seine.'

'Oh my God! No.'

'Oh my God! Yes.'

'She killed herself?'

'That is usually what happens when people throw themselves into a river, is it not?'

'But why? Why?'

Madame Cochet shrugged expressively. 'Who knows?' She looked hard at Isabella. 'You have no suggestion?'

'I? No, none.'

And yet she was remembering how the girl had wept when told that her fellow lodger was going away with a man. She remembered too that a failed artist had taken a similar path to oblivion after living at that same apartment. Perhaps the example had influenced Juliette in her choice of an exit from this life.

'I am so sorry.'

'As we all were. Such a nice young girl. But now she is almost forgotten. It is the way of the world.'

So there was no going back to the old lodgings for Isabella. She looked around and found a rather better ground-floor apartment in a different part of Paris. Even if the other place had been available she would not have wished to return to it. It would have been haunted by the dead girl, just one of an unending succession of misfits swallowed by that ever-hungry, never-sated river.

She paid a second visit to the Moulin Rouge the next morning. Madame Cochet had agreed, none too eagerly, to give her the chance to re-establish herself as a favourite with the public.

'You will need some practice, as I have said. And exercise to get fit. We will see how it goes.'

It did not go too well at first. It was so long since she had danced, and no one could hope to start again at the point where they had left off. It was not only some of the skill that had been lost but the stamina also. She became tired very quickly; her legs ached and she became short of breath. But she persevered and gradually it came back; not perhaps quite all the old panache but sufficient for Madame Cochet to give her approval.

'You have worked hard and I think next week we may introduce you to an audience.'

So the posters went up: 'Return of L'Anglaise!' There was the Toulouse-Lautrec picture of her too; the one she so disliked.

'Let us hope,' Madame Cochet said, 'that they have not forgotten you. You were a favourite before you left, but a year is a long time. However, we shall see.'

She need have had no qualms. L'Anglaise had not been forgotten. It was as though the patrons of the Moulin Rouge had been waiting expectantly for her return. They came and were charmed again.

Madame Cochet was delighted, though somewhat surprised.

'I hardly expected it. I imagined they would have forgotten you. But apparently not. I wonder what it is about you that draws them to you. It cannot be because you are English. So what is it?'

This was a question that Isabella herself could not answer. She just had to accept the fact that she pleased the audiences and thank her lucky stars that it was so.

It was hardly to be expected that her return would be welcomed by all the other performers. There were a few who resented the fact that she could go away and come back just when it suited her. One of these was a girl named Colette who was rather tall and not particularly attractive. She would make snide remarks about foreign intruders which were obviously aimed at one English performer. The fact that Isabella ignored all this and refused to be drawn into any retaliation merely added to the other girl's resentment. For the present, however, the antagonism remained verbal, and sotto voce at that. So no harm was done.

One day an old acquaintance of Isabella's turned up. It was Monsieur Henri Dupin, the man who had originally brought her to France. She had seen him fairly frequently during the first period of her engagement at the Moulin Rouge, but this was the first encounter with him since her return from Germany.

He was as dapper as ever and greeted her with effusion.

'So you are back. That is good. You have been sorely missed. It was very wicked of you to go off like that and leave us mourning. However, now you are here again and all is well.'

She told him she was pleased to be back. And she was, in a way. She loved performing before an audience and the applause was music to her ears. Though she had not really missed it in those early days and months with Otto she had always felt as though there were something that she had lost by running away with him.

'That man you were with in England,' Dupin said. 'What was his name? I have forgotten.'

'Gerald Hardacre.'

'Ah yes. Do you ever hear from him?'

'Never. We lost touch when I left England. I am not even sure whether he is still alive.'

'No? Well, perhaps it was best to make a clean break.'

'I think so.'

She seldom thought of Gerald now. Yet it was he who had set her on the road to her present occupation. How long ago it seemed now. She was only seventeen at the time when he persuaded her to run away with him, and people might say it had been an evil thing to do, since it was surely to serve his own ends, but she did not regret anything. Life for her might have been horribly dull if he had not appeared on the scene. And surely it was better to be dead than dull.

Dupin had never made any attempt to make their relationship anything but a purely business one. He had acted more like a father than a prospective lover, though a very different kind of father from the real one, that country business man who had tried to bring her back to the family home and had wept when she refused.

She thought of two others in the family – her sisters. They would be grown up now and married perhaps to dull husbands with dull jobs. Did they ever speak of her, any of them back there in England, or was she regarded as an outcast, even a sinner, not to be mentioned in respectable company? It rather amused her to think so. Of one thing she was certain: she had no desire to return to the bosom of her family. It would, she imagined, be a somewhat chilly bosom for a returning prodigal such as she.

Anyway, it would never happen. She was sure of that.

Monsieur Dupin had been watching her closely. He seemed to be reading her mind, for he said: 'Your family in England. Have you ever had any desire to return to them?'

'Never.'

'Would they, do you suppose, approve of what you are doing?'

'I doubt it. I ran away, you see. My sisters might envy me. They might even wish they had the courage to do the same. My father made every effort to persuade me to return home.'

'And of course you refused.'

'Yes.'

'Your father. What is he?'

She hesitated, debating in her mind whether to tell the truth or invent some distinguished profession. But truth prevailed.

'He is an ironmonger.'

Monsieur Dupin looked as if he wanted to laugh but was making a valiant effort to suppress the inclination.

'An ironmonger?'

'In a small village.'

'You amaze me.'

'Well, now you know my dark secret. But please don't spread it around.'

'I shall be an oyster,' Dupin promised.

23

ACCIDENT

It was the girl named Colette who was instrumental in bringing Isabella's present stint as a dancer at the Moulin Rouge to a halt. Whether it was by design or accident no one could be certain. She herself vehemently denied any premeditation, but of course she would be bound to do so, and bearing in mind her hostility to L'Anglaise, not everyone believed her.

It happened when both were hurrying to the head of a short stairway. They reached it almost together and collided with each other. The result was that Isabella went tumbling down the stairs while Colette managed to remain at the top. The sound of an ankle bone breaking was distinctly audible and even more so the cry of pain given by the victim.

Others were soon on the scene. She was lifted up but could stand only on one foot. Madame Cochet was summoned to the scene of the accident, if accident it was, and was devastated. Even a sprained ankle would have been bad enough, but if, as had to be feared, this was a broken one, it was a disaster.

The victim was taken without delay to a hospital where the worst fears were confirmed: the ankle was indeed broken.

It could not, Madame Cochet said, have happened at a more inconvenient time. Where was she to find a replacement at short notice for L'Anglaise? How long, moreover, would it take for the ankle to heal?

The surgeon was not hopeful. It would be a lengthy process at best. It was not a simple fracture; by no means so. It was multiple; he had seldom had to deal with a worse case. Pressed by Madame Cochet to give an estimate of just how long it would be before the victim was able to dance again, he shook his head.

'To dance? Not for many months.' He did not add 'if ever' but it was there to be read in his expression.

So, instead of appearing on stage at the Moulin Rouge Isabella lay in a hospital bed in a crowded ward, feeling the pain in her ankle and worrying about the future. Suddenly everything, from appearing to be as good as it could possibly be, had become horribly uncertain.

One cheerful note was struck by the appearance of Monsieur Henri Dupin. He came to offer his condolences.

'Such a misfortune. Who could have foreseen such a thing? However, I am sure you will soon be back on your feet. Both of them. And all will be well. Meanwhile, my dear, you are not to bother your head about expenses. I personally will see to all that.'

She thanked him. It took a weight off her mind; for obviously she would be earning nothing while she was out of action. She had the jewellery in the bank deposit of course, but she would have had to trust an agent to handle any of that, and this she did not wish to do.

Sometimes she wondered whether it had really been an accident, that collision with Colette. She knew that the girl disliked her; was perhaps jealous because of the interest taken in her and the publicity she received. So maybe she had engineered that collision at the top of the stairs with the intention of sending her rival tumbling down. She could not, of course, have foreseen the result of the fall and perhaps had never had in her mind anything quite so disastrous. It was noticeable, however, that she had not paid a visit to offer her condolences. But, one way or another, what difference did it make? The damage was done and only time could undo it.

After a day or two she had become quite a celebrity in the ward. 'A dancer from the Moulin Rouge! Fancy that! And English too!'

The nurses treated her with the respect due to such a person and the surgeon paid her more attention than might have been normal. At least, so she believed. She was, after all, even lying in a hospital bed, very beautiful, and he was male and young enough to be susceptible to feminine charm.

When he examined her ankle it seemed to her that he uncovered more of her leg than was strictly necessary; but then again he was young and the leg was one of the shapeliest ever put on show at the Moulin Rouge.

As things turned out the fracture was less serious than the surgeon had initially suggested. Soon she was in a wheelchair and, since the weather was warm and fine, she was allowed to sit out in the hospital garden; which was far more pleasant than lying in bed in the ward. Here again Dr Madelin, as the young surgeon's name was, made it his business to visit her.

'You are doing very well,' he assured her. 'Soon we will have you walking. With crutches at first, of course. No dancing yet, I am afraid, but all in good time. Be patient. Rome was not built in a day, so I have been told.'

She had the impression that he was talking for the sake of talking; reluctant to hurry away, though he must have had plenty of other patients to attend to.

She was pleased nevertheless to have him assure her that the ankle was progressing well. She was impatient to be walking on it as the preliminary to an eventual resumption of dancing. She missed the atmosphere of the theatre and the applause from a crowded house, the feeling that she had all these people in the palm of her hand, or perhaps more accurately, at her feet.

It appeared that the original somewhat depressing prognosis had been rather exaggerated. The fracture turned out to be far less serious than Dr Madelin had suggested, and his later and more encouraging words were nearer the truth. The patient was indeed soon walking with the aid of crutches, and from there she progressed to a stick.

When finally she was able to throw the stick away and stand, as it were, on her own two feet, it might have been imagined that she would be in a very short space of time back on stage delighting audiences with her truly magical dancing.

So it might have been, but for one thing: she had a limp.

'Perhaps it will wear off,' Madame Cochet suggested.

But of course it was not the kind of thing that would wear off. It was permanent.

For Isabella it was a disaster. It was the end of her career on the stage, for who ever heard of a professional dancer with a limp?

Madame Cochet was sympathetic. 'Such a tragedy for one so talented. Who would have imagined it? What will you do now?'

It was a question Isabella had asked herself and had found no answer. She had no profession but that of a dancer, and now that was finished.

'Would it not be possible for you to go back to England?'

The thought had occurred to her, but she had rejected it out of hand. How could she ever bring herself to go crawling back to the family like a prodigal daughter? It would be an admission of defeat, a confession that she had been a fool to run away. Any course of action would be preferable to that.

It was not as if she were destitute either. She had some money and there were the jewels that Otto had given her lying in a deposit box in a Paris bank. She had no idea how much they were worth but it had to be a considerable sum, for he had been quite profligate in those days and bought only the most expensive offerings for the woman he loved. So the future was not entirely bleak, and she might perhaps find employment of some kind, though she had no idea what. Unfortunately experience of any but that which was now out of the question.

Six months later she still had not found a job, but she was no longer alone. She was living with a man.

24

JACQUES MAURAT

Though it might have been more accurate to say that the man was living with her, since it was her apartment that was accommodating the two of them.

It was a chance meeting that had brought them together. She was sitting by herself at a small table in a bar where she had gone more for the sake of some human company than the glass of wine which she had in front of her and was very slowly consuming. She did not notice the man approaching, and he was almost at her elbow when she heard his voice.

'Would it be an intrusion if I were to share this table with Madame?'

He had one hand on the back of a vacant chair and a glass of what might have been brandy in the other. He was a man of medium height wearing a dark grey suit and a hat which he removed at once. His hair was black and receding slightly and he had side-whiskers and a neatly-trimmed moustache but no beard. A stiff white collar looked as if it had been specifically designed for the purpose of supporting his head, since it reached almost to his ears. In age he might have been somewhere between forty and forty-five. He was neither handsome nor ugly, but had the kind of face that might have been forgotten as soon as it disappeared from sight. He had a soft voice which gave the impression that he was imparting some confidential information.

Isabella gave a little nod of the head to indicate that he was free to use the chair. She was in fact rather glad to have someone sitting there, since it made her feel less conspicuous. She had been aware of some curious glances in her direction. A young woman as attractive as she was drinking alone in a bar could hardly avoid rousing some unwanted interest.

'It is,' the man said, 'a pleasant evening.'

Isabella agreed that it was.

The man took a sip of whatever it was in his glass, put the glass down and said: 'Pardon my asking, Madame, but haven't we met somewhere before?'

'No,' she said, 'I don't think so. In fact I am sure we have not.'

'And yet I feel I have seen you somewhere. If I may take the liberty of saying so, yours is not a face one could easily forget. So where can it have been?'

He appeared to be genuinely convinced that he had seen

her before, and she believed he was not inventing a previous encounter as an opening gambit. So could he have seen her without her seeing him? The answer should have been obvious at once.

'The Moulin Rouge?'

He slapped his forehead with the flat of his hand. 'But of course. You are L'Anglaise. How could I not have realised it at once?'

'So you go to the Moulin Rouge?'

'Now and then. But I have not seen you there lately.'

'And you never will again.'

He looked surprised. 'No? Why is that?'

'I can no longer dance. An accident. My ankle was broken and it has never healed properly. The fact is, I limp.'

'Oh, what a misfortune. And to happen to someone like you who was so brilliant a performer. I am desolated. It is a tragedy.'

She thought he was reacting a shade too extravagantly, but he did seem genuinely concerned, which made her inclined to regard him with some favour. Having thus, as it were, broken the ice they became more communicative. He introduced himself as Jacques Maurat and told her that he was a financial consultant. He had, so he said, several important clients, though he did not name them.

After this they got on very well together. They had more drinks, which he paid for, and she told him her name was Isabella Foster. She also told him that she had lost all contact with her family and had never been back home since leaving. He thought this rather sad. He himself was an orphan and had never had any family to call his own.

Later in the evening when she said it was time to return to her apartment he insisted on escorting her there, since it was not safe for a single woman to be out on the streets at that time of night. He was at present living in a hotel, since he had recently sold his own house and was looking around for a suitable replacement.

When they reached her apartment, which was not far distant, she thought he might expect to be invited in; and she almost did so but decided against it. Nevertheless, he seemed unwilling, now that he had made her acquaintance, to leave it at that, and he suggested that perhaps they might meet again, since for him at least it had been such an enjoyable evening.

Alarm-bells started ringing in her head, but they were faint and she ignored them. She was too much alone now that she had left the Moulin Rouge, and she clutched at the chance of some relief from this isolation. Moreover, Monsieur Jacques Maurat was undoubtedly quite a charming man and certainly not old. What harm then could there be in agreeing to meet him again? If on a second encounter she discovered that they really had nothing in common there need never be a third. Nothing would be lost.

So she said: 'Yes, I think that might be rather pleasant.'

And thus it was arranged. He said he could not meet her the next day because he had some important business to transact. But the day after that, if it was convenient for her?

She said it was. And that was that.

25

WHO ELSE?

In the company of Jacques Maurat Isabella got to see more of Paris than she had ever done before. He became her guide and, incidentally, her lover. It was really most convenient; at least for him, since, having sold his house and having not yet acquired a replacement, he had been forced to live in a hotel room while he looked around.

Apparently, after moving in with Isabella, he had stopped looking around, for he made no further mention to her of any such activity. It appeared also that his business as a financial consultant did not take up a great deal of his time, though he did now and then set out with a briefcase and return only late in the day. She assumed that this was when he went to see his clients, but she asked no questions.

He seemed to have sufficient money and made an offer to

contribute to the running expenses of the apartment. This was soon after he moved in.

'We must come to some arrangement,' he said. 'I must put my share in the pot.'

Oddly enough, he made no further mention of this, and she supposed it had slipped his mind. She hesitated to remind him of the promise, and after all, the expense was very little greater than when she had had the place to herself, so why bother? She noticed that his wardrobe was well stocked, for he brought with him two large portmanteaus and later a trunk was delivered.

He was really something of a dandy and had quite a variety of suits. But she supposed he needed to be well-dressed when he went to meet his clients, since they would hardly have been favourably impressed by a financial consultant who looked like a tramp.

There was one great advantage of having a profession that left him with so much free time. He was in consequence able to act as her guide to those parts of Paris that she had never previously visited. He was amazed that she had never set foot on the Île de la Cité.

'My dear lady, it is the very heart of Paris. So you have never seen the Cathedral of Notre Dame?'

She admitted with some shame that she had not.

'But you must have read Victor Hugo's novel in which the hunchback Quasimodo appears.'

She shook her head, feeling very ignorant. For though

they had been taught French at Miss Lowther's school for young ladies they had been introduced to scarcely any French literature.

'Well, well! It seems there is much to show you in this fair city.'

This, in the weeks and months that followed, he proceeded to do, proving himself a knowledgeable guide. One day he even hired a boat and took her for a row on the Seine; demonstrating that he was no mean hand with the oars. Another day they hired an open landau and took a turn along the Avenue des Champs-Elysée. The sun shone and there were quite a number of horse-riders to be seen.

'It is amazing,' Maurat remarked, 'that one sunny day can discover so many citizens with no work to do.'

'Like us.'

He smiled. 'As you say. Like us.'

This period, she reflected, was the most enjoyable she had experienced since the breaking of her ankle. Sometimes she wondered quite how long it would last; for, looking back, it seemed that just when things appeared to be going well there would come some incident to bring the good time to an end. But since one could never see into the future there was really nothing one could do to avoid these sudden changes in fortune. Therefore there was no sense in bothering one's head about possible disasters waiting round the corner. If they happened, they happened, and that was all there was to it.

She wondered whether Jacques had had similar experiences. She knew nothing about his life before that first encounter in the bar. He had revealed nothing of importance to her, and she had asked no questions. If there were any dark secrets back there she did not wish to hear about them. There was much to be said for a policy of leaving well alone.

It was a policy he too appeared to be observing. He knew something of her past of course. He knew that she had been a dancer at the Moulin-Rouge, but he did not know how she, an English girl, had come to be there. Nor did he know anything of that year-long gap in her career when she had been with Otto in Germany. She felt no inclination to speak of that to anyone.

In the end, however, it was Jacques who broke the unstated rule and asked a personal question. He did so hesitantly, admitting that it was something that had bothered him a little. It was, he said, apparent that since leaving the Moulin Rouge she had had no paid employment; yet it was also apparent that she had money. Otherwise how could she afford to rent an apartment in that part of the city and purchase the necessities of life?

She gave a laugh, though it sounded more than a little forced. 'Don't you think that is my business?'

'And none of mine? Yes, I admit it. And of course you are in no way obliged to tell me. But as one who is more than a little interested in your welfare and has much experience of financial matters, it occurs to me that I might be able to help in some way. If help is needed.'

'Ah, you think I am incapable of dealing efficiently with money matters and that you might be able to put me on the right track. Is that it?'

She thought he seemed a little put out by her reaction to his inquiry, for he frowned slightly. When he answered it was with a degree of acidity.

'You are bound to tell me nothing if you do not wish to do so. I am trying to be helpful, but of course if you need no help, so be it.'

She hastened to smooth out any ruffling of his feathers she might have caused; for the truth was that she could not be sure she was managing her finances in the most sensible way.

'Please,' she said, 'don't be offended. As a matter of fact I should be grateful for some advice from an expert.'

He assured her that he was not at all offended and he would be delighted to help her in any way he could.

'Very well then. You would like to know how I'm managing to exist now that I have no job. The answer is simple: I'm living on my jewels.'

He looked puzzled. 'Perhaps you had better give me a little more detail. I am not quite sure I understand.'

'As I said, it is quite simple. I have some jewellery deposited in a bank. When I need money I sell a piece.

Actually so far I've only had to part with one – a bracelet. It will keep me going for a while yet. The jewels were given to me by a certain person who was very, very rich. And still is, I imagine. I can assure you that whatever he bought for me was certainly not trash.'

She suddenly became aware of the expression on Maurat's face. It could only be described as one of horror.

'So this is how you intend to live? By selling your jewellery, piece by piece.'

'What else can I do? I have no alternative.'

'And when you eventually come to the end of this source of income. What then?'

'Oh,' she said, 'that will not be for a long time yet.'

But he had touched a nerve. This was a kind of spectre that she tried to keep shut away, but which now and then broke out to haunt her. What would she do when the well ran dry?

'A long time,' he said. 'Yes, maybe. But how long? And how long will you live? It will be a race between the two: your life and the jewels. Which will have the more stamina?'

'I know, I know. You mustn't suppose I haven't thought about it. I have. But what can I do? Are you suggesting I should seek work? I have no training for anything except dancing. And that is no longer possible.'

He looked at her and gave a little shake of the head. 'My dear, my dear! How ignorant you must be of financial matters, and how fortunate that you have me to advise you. Don't you see that your jewels can be converted into a source of regular income that will last indefinitely?'

'No. Tell me how.'

'Why, all you have to do is sell them and invest the proceeds. You could put the lot on deposit in a bank and draw the interest at regular intervals.'

'Oh,' she said, 'how stupid of me. I never thought of that. And you think the interest would be enough to live on?'

'That of course would depend on how much you got for the jewels. But there is a more profitable way of investing the money.'

'Tell me.'

'You could buy shares in a company. Then you would be paid dividends which, if you chose the right company would amount to much more than your interest from any bank.'

'But I know nothing about that sort of business. I wouldn't know how to set about buying these things you call shares. I'm completely ignorant of all that.'

Maurat smiled. 'Of course you are, my dear. That is why you would need to have an adviser. Someone whose business it is to handle this kind of thing.'

She looked at him with raised eyebrows. 'You?'

'Who else?'

26

MONEY MATTERS

One of the first things he told her was that she had almost certainly been underpaid for the first piece of jewellery she had sold.

'You took it to a jeweller and accepted just what he offered for it?'

She admitted that she had. 'What else could I have done?'

'You should have haggled. He would have expected you to. He must have been agreeably surprised when you walked away with his opening bid with no attempt to get more.'

'You really think so?'

'I am sure of it.'

'And yet he seemed such a pleasant obliging man.'

'He would. All part of the game.'

She felt stupid and also annoyed to think that she had been duped. And the fact was that she doubted whether she could ever become an adept haggler. It was just not her line.

Maurat appeared to read her mind. 'You don't think you can do it, do you?'

'No, I don't.'

'So would you like me to handle that part of the business as well?'

It seemed the obvious solution to the problem. She did not doubt for a moment that he would get a better price for her jewellery than she could ever have obtained herself. So she accepted his offer without hesitation, reflecting how fortunate it was that she should have someone with so much knowledge of financial matters to advise her. Left to herself she would gradually have sold all her pot of gold for far less than its true value and might in not so very many years have had to sell it all merely to survive.

Maurat was amazed when he saw how much there was after she had taken it from the bank. Back in the apartment she spread out the collection on a table where the diamonds glittered and the emeralds and sapphires shone in their golden settings. There were rings, brooches, necklaces and bracelets, all of the finest quality. Otto had undoubtedly been lavish with his gifts, never reckoning the cost.

'Well,' Maurat said, 'you are certainly not destitute. I never imagined there would be so much.'

He suggested that the best plan would be to take each piece separately to a different jeweller. There was no lack of choice in a city the size of Paris. Isabella agreed. She was willing to follow his advice, since she had come to put her trust in his experience.

She did not love him. There had been only one man in her life whom she had truly loved, and he was probably now married to a princess. But Jacques was a pleasant companion and she would have felt lost without him.

When he went to a jeweller she accompanied him. They would spend a little time inspecting the jewellery on display in order to get some idea of the price being asked for pieces similar to the one they wished to sell. One had of course to allow for the jeweller's profit, but it was a way of determining some approximation to the value of their own offering.

As soon as the jeweller understood that they were selling rather than buying he would take them into a private room at the rear of the shop where he would examine the object very closely with the aid of an eyeglass and then make an offer, which Maurat would treat with contempt. The bargaining would then go on for some time, and Maurat might pretend to lose patience, pick up the bracelet or whatever it was and get as far as the door before being called back to receive a somewhat higher offer. It was all a game of wits which Isabella watched without ever uttering a word.

Maurat always insisted on payment in cash, and the amount of francs in high denomination notes that they had in the apartment grew steadily larger. They stowed the paper money in various hiding-places until one day they put all, but a certain quantity retained to cover living expenses for the next few months, in a canvas bag and set off in a cab for the Paris Bourse. Here in a rather dusty office the money was handed over and a rather bemused Isabella signed her name in various places and finally came away with a very official-looking document which Maurat assured her was as good as money in the bank.

'It means,' he said, 'that you are now a shareholder in a company which is one of the most successful to be found. From now on you are free of any financial worries and you can set your mind at rest in that regard.'

She was rather bemused by it all, but she had to take his word for this. And indeed it soon appeared that he had been speaking nothing but the truth, as from time to time there would arrive in the post a piece of paper with some figures and her name on it which she would take to the bank and exchange for cash.

She was grateful to Jacques for sorting matters out for her. Now she need have no more qualms concerning the future: she had a steady income, a comfortable apartment and a man to take care of her. It was regrettable that her career at the Moulin Rouge had come to an untimely end, but it could in any case not have gone on for ever, so why shed tears about it?

She still knew very little about Maurat. She asked no questions, but now and then he would let fall a snippet of information; like the fact that he was not a native Parisian. He had been born in a small town in Normandy and had come to Paris as a young man to seek his fortune.

'And have you found it?'

He smiled at this. 'I think now I have.'

He was still making no contribution to their living expenses, but she was not bothered about this and made no demands. Occasionally he would ask for a small loan to tide him over a sticky patch, and she concluded that one of his clients in the financial consultancy line had not paid up or perhaps had taken his custom elsewhere. There could hardly have been many of them anyway; otherwise he would not have had so much time to be with her.

She rather doubted that story of his having sold a house. He had never told her where it was or anything else about it. And what had happened to all the money he received for it? There probably had never been a house but was just a harmless piece of fiction.

27

PARTING

Five years passed and she wondered just where they had gone. Nothing much seemed to have happened in the course of those years. She was still living with Jacques Maurat, or, again to be more precise, he was still living with her. At first he had frequently acted as a guide to Paris, and she had enjoyed these outings. There had been evenings at the theatre too, though never the Moulin Rouge. But these, like the outings, had gradually been given up and life had really become somewhat dull. Sometimes it occurred to her that they were like an old married couple between whom all passion had been spent and living was just a changeless routine.

When she looked in a mirror she thought she could detect the telltale signs of ageing: little wrinkles here and there, a thickening below the chin, maybe even a hint of grey hair. She hated it. Other people grew old. She had never faced the certainty that it must happen to her also.

Yet she was still scarcely thirty.

Jacques was of course a good deal older, though he had never revealed his exact age and she had never asked him to. And with men perhaps it did not matter so much.

What really did matter, and indeed was in the nature of a bombshell, was that one morning she found him packing a portmanteau. When she asked him why he was doing it he answered briefly without looking at her.

'I'm leaving.'

She could not believe he was serious. It had to be some ridiculous kind of joke, though it was difficult to detect the humour in it.

'What is this nonsense?' she demanded.

Again he did not look at her, but just went on with the packing, carefully folding the clothes and stowing them away.

'It's not nonsense. I've been living with you too long. I think we've both become tired of it. Isn't that so?'

'And so you suddenly decide to walk out on me? Is that it?'

'I've been thinking about it for some time.'

'So why did you never mention it to me? Did you think I wouldn't be interested? That it was no concern of mine?'

He made no answer to that. He had not once turned to look at her. She was talking to the back of his head. And suddenly she knew what he was not admitting; the true reason for this sudden decision to walk out on her. Perhaps it was not so very sudden after all. Perhaps it had been building up for quite a while and only now had he found the nerve to bring things to a head.

'It's another woman, isn't it?'

He did not reply at once, but his hands had stopped moving, as if the question had arrested them in the carrying out of some nefarious act.

She had to repeat the question before she could get an answer.

'Isn't it?'

Then suddenly he turned and looked at her and snapped the answer that she had been demanding.

'Yes, it is.'

Though she had guessed correctly, the confirmation when it came was still a shock. It was so unexpected. She had imagined he was perfectly contented living with her and that their relationship would continue indefinitely. Now, abruptly, it was ended. She would be alone again. Though she had never loved Jacques she had liked him well enough, and there had never been any friction between them. Theirs had been a relationship remarkably free from disputes of any serious nature. There had been no bickering, none of those heated arguments that so often marred the lives of married couples. So why did he have to look elsewhere?

It angered her. So much so that at that moment she felt a sudden urge to hit him and thus give vent to her resentment by physical means. But she resisted the impulse. It would serve no useful purpose to lose control of herself. Instead she just said bitterly:

'I suppose she is more attractive than me?'

His answer surprised her.

'No,' he said. 'How could she be?'

'Then why?'

He shrugged as only a Frenchman could. 'It is useless to try to explain.'

He closed the portmanteau and fastened it. He took his overcoat from the wardrobe and put it on; then picked up the bag.

'I shall take this with me. The trunk will be called for later. I have already packed it. There is nothing of yours in it.'

His coolness exasperated her. Again she had the urge to strike him and again resisted it. He seemed to guess what was in her mind and shrugged again.

'You may hit me if you wish. Perhaps I deserve it. But it would not alter the situation.'

'I would rather not dirty my hand.'

He gave a little laugh. 'So I am dirt now, am I? Well, that's the way it goes. You would not, I imagine, wish me to kiss you goodbye.'

'Go,' she said. 'I never wish to see you again.'

In the hallway he picked up his hat and his stick. He opened the door and was gone.

28
TROUBLE

It was like the time before she had met Maurat. It was like it and yet different, because now she was older and she had the memory of how much better it had been having someone with whom to share the apartment; a companion to talk to and ask for help when she needed it. Time passed so slowly, pointlessly. There seemed to be no purpose in living; it was just one empty day after another.

She thought of visiting the Moulin Rouge, but then thought better of it. She could not be sure that Madame Cochet was still there; and even if she was, whether she would wish to renew the acquaintance. What would they have to say to each other?

She could have visited the places to which Maurat had taken her when he had been widening her knowledge of Paris; but there would have been no pleasure in it now. One needed a companion, and she had none.

One day when she was out shopping she caught sight of him with a woman on his arm. The woman, no doubt. She was wearing a wide-brimmed hat adorned with artificial roses, and when she turned her head it was possible to see that she was of a dark complexion and the pouting lips might have indicated a sulky nature. She was certainly young, but her figure was dumpy and it was difficult to see what had attracted Maurat to her, apart from her youth. But of course it was impossible to see with another person's eyes; especially when that other person was of a different sex.

Isabella had quickly withdrawn into the cover of a shop doorway and Maurat had not even glanced in her direction. He was talking to the girl and seemed to be suggesting something with which she was disagreeing. Isabella could see that the man had put a hand on her arm and that she pulled the arm away with a pettish gesture. She also said something which Isabella could not hear.

Then they were gone and she saw no more of them. Indeed, as things turned out she was never again to see the girl who had taken her place in Jacques Maurat's life.

There was one thing for which she had to thank Maurat: he had put her finances on a firm footing. She now had no worries about the future in that respect, since the little slips of printed paper continued to arrive at regular intervals and were changed at the bank for a pleasing amount of cash.

But she would have been happier if she had had a companion. First there had been Gerald Hardacre, then Juliette LeBlanc, then the best of all, Otto Axter-Mandel, and finally Jacques Maurat. Now there was no one.

She decided that what she needed was some activity to pass the time. She tried knitting, but gave it up almost immediately. Crochet lasted a little longer but then went the same way. She bought a tin of paints and some brushes and attempted water-colour painting but soon discovered that she had no talent whatever in this line. Her artistic gifts had all been in the dance, and that was now denied her.

She had no friends. She scarcely knew the people who lived next door and she had no desire to make their acquaintance. She did a lot of reading. She browsed through secondhand bookshops and open-air stalls and carried her purchases back home in a shopping-basket. She read in bed by the light of a candle and often fell asleep, to wake up hours later to find the candle burnt out and the room in darkness.

So the days passed, and the weeks and the months, with nothing to stir the blood or relieve the monotony. Sometimes she thought of the family in England she had left behind her all those years ago; but she felt no desire to return. It would be humiliating. She could imagine the things that would be said about her. At the height of her success on the stage she might have faced them all, but not now that this was all behind her. No; she would never go back.

There came a day when boredom was banished; though she would have been happier if the banishment had never been effected in such a way. A thousand times better any amount of boredom than this.

It was autumn; late in the evening. There had been rain earlier but now it had stopped, leaving a chill in the air, and she had lighted a fire in the sitting-room. She loved fires. You could sit by them, warming your feet and watching the coals burn. Sometimes there would be a hiss and a flame would shoot out like a demon that had been suddenly released from prison. You could picture all sorts of things in the glowing embers of an open fire; fanciful pictures coming and going. She was doing just this on that fateful evening. You could also fall asleep in an armchair; as she did too.

The knocking seemed at first merely to be part of a dream she was having, and it did not immediately awaken her. But then she came out of her dreamland and back to reality. Moreover, the reality was that someone was hammering as if in a frenzy on the front door.

She did not go at once to open it. It was as if she had a

premonition that opening the door could mean letting in something evil.

The fire had burnt low and she felt cold. It was late now, so who could possibly be paying a call on her at that time of night?

The knocking continued with scarcely any abatement. Indeed, it seemed to become even more frenzied. She wondered who it could be and she could think of only one person who could be calling on her at that hour: Jacques.

But why? She had not seen him since that afternoon when he had been with the girl. So why, if indeed it were he, would he be coming to her now?

The knocking continued with more insistence. Summoning up her courage she went into the dimly lit hallway and unlocked the door.

As soon as she opened it the man rushed in and slammed it shut behind him before turning the key in the lock.

She saw at once that it was indeed Jacques Maurat, but with neither hat nor coat. She began to say something, but he brushed past her and went into the room where she had been dozing by the fire.

There was an oil-lamp on the table and by its light she could now see him clearly and was shocked by what she saw.

There was a red stain on his hands and on his jacket; stain that she guessed had not been made by paint.

He had collapsed rather than sat down in the chair she

had been sitting in; and now he buried his face in his hands so that some of the crimson stain was transferred to his cheeks. His shoulders were shaking as if with an ague, and he seemed to be weeping.

She could not move. She stood there looking down at him and wondering what had happened and what it was he had been running from. She did not dare to ask.

When he spoke the words were so faint as to be almost inaudible. They seemed to stick in his throat. But she heard them and wished she had not.

'I've killed her.'

She was stunned. For a few moments the words simply did not make sense to her. They were just words: meaningless. Then he repeated them.

'I've killed her.'

And this time the full import of them got through to her. He was talking about the girl she had seen him with in the street. It was her blood staining his hands, his clothing, his face.

But why? Why would he wish to kill her?

Then, as if in answer to the question she had not voiced, he said: 'She goaded me. She was always doing it. She never did anything I asked of her. She sneered at me; called me an old man, a dodderer. It went on and on, day after day. I lost my temper. There was this knife, a cook's knife. I picked it up and stabbed her with it. She screamed. I went on stabbing, and then she was on the floor, not screaming any more; not making a sound; not moving; just lying there.'

He was mumbling now. He seemed to have lost the thread of what he was saying. And then his shoulders began to shake and he was sobbing again.

She stood there, looking down at him, and the full import of what he had said gradually revealed itself to her. She began to realise just how this must affect her. The moment he stepped through that doorway into the hall he had brought trouble for her. She saw it so clearly now: he had involved her in this crime he had committed.

It was so unfair. He had walked out on her when it suited him to do so, throwing her over for someone younger who had caught his fancy; and now, when that relationship had ended in tragedy, he had come back here for refuge.

But she would not let him do this to her. Why should she? She owed him nothing. He had treated her as badly as any man could, and now in this extremity he had come to her to provide a refuge for him. But that she would not do.

'You must go,' she said. 'You cannot stay here.'

He turned his head and looked at her, his face smeared with the blood from his hands and streaked now with the tears he had shed.

'But where else can I go? You can't throw me out. There is nowhere but here. For pity's sake, Bella!'

When he called her that it touched a nerve, and she knew that she had lost. She knew that she could not get rid of him. He had brought his trouble to her and now it was her trouble too.

'Oh, God!' she said. 'Why did we ever have to meet?'

29

WAITING

The days passed. Nerve-tingling days when the least sound was like a portent, a thing of ill omen.

Maurat was a wreck. He seemed to be trembling all the time, and the least sound startled him. He had washed the blood from his hands and face, and they had tried to wash it out of his clothes but without success; the stain was still there. Isabella had to go out to buy food, though he begged her not to go. He was fearful of being left alone. But she wanted to get away from the confines of the apartment, if only for a short while.

'You will come back?' he said, tugging at her arm. 'You won't leave me?'

She broke away from him, repelled by his touch as by something unclean. 'Where would I go? This is my home.'

And she thought: 'It is a home contaminated by this thing, this murderer, who has involved me in his crime.'

*

In a shop she overheard two women talking. She caught snatches of their conversation.

'Such a young girl—'

'Blood everywhere, they say—'

'An older man—'

'Police haven't found him yet—'

'But they will. Murder will out—'

'Must be hiding somewhere—'

She did not need to be told what they were discussing. It would be in the papers, of course. She could have bought one and read about it. But what good would that do?

He was waiting impatiently for her when she entered the apartment, using her key in the lock of the front door.

'You've been a long time.' It was as though he were accusing her of wrong-doing. 'I was beginning to think you'd gone to them.'

He did not say whom he meant by 'them', but she knew. He was afraid she might have informed the police; told them where they could find the man they were seeking. Maybe she should have done just that, for her own sake. For was she not committing a crime by harbouring him?

'The body has been discovered,' she said. 'People are talking about it. You can't stay here, you know.'

'But where can I go?'

'Suppose you were to slip away after dark, leave Paris, get yourself out into the country, use a different name—'

She could tell that the mere suggestion frightened him. He was fearful of leaving the apartment which had become a kind of sanctuary for him.

'You want to get rid of me, don't you?'

She answered in exasperation: 'Well, of course I do. Don't you see you're a threat to me? You've involved me in a crime I didn't commit.'

'There was nowhere else to go.'

'There was everywhere else. But you had to bring this trouble on me. Why? Why?'

He had no answer to that.

30

INTERROGATION

They came early one morning, heralded by thunderous knocking on the front door.

Maurat clutched Isabella's arm. 'It's them. Don't let them in. Don't let them in.'

'You fool,' she said. 'If I don't open the door they'll break it down.'

She wrenched her arm away from him and walked into the hallway just as another spate of knocking shook the door. She turned the key and opened the door, and they came in at once, pushing her in front of them like a wave casting some piece of flotsam up on a beach.

There were four of them; two in plain clothes and two in uniform. One of the plain clothes officers showed her a card of some kind, but she had no time to read what was on it.

'Monsieur Maurat is here?' he said. But he did not wait for a reply. It was a statement rather than a question.

He brushed past her and the others followed, one of them closing the door behind him.

They found Maurat hiding under a bed. He must have been out of his senses to imagine he could avoid being discovered in that way.

They arrested Isabella also; as an accessory.

There was a horse-drawn van waiting in the street outside. It had little windows with bars on them. Isabella and Maurat were bundled into it while one of the plain clothes officers locked the door of the apartment and pocketed the key. She heard the driver of the van whip the horses and felt the vibration as the wheels rattled over the cobbles.

Maurat was huddled in a corner and shaking as if with a fever, an expression of terror on his face. He seemed already to be anticipating what the end of the procedure must inevitably be for him. He had been a smart, self-possessed man, very full of his own importance, but it was evident now that he lacked courage when it came to the point.

Isabella was frightened too; for who would not be in such a situation; but she refused to show it. Perhaps it was the anger in her that suppressed the terror; for she was certainly angry, and the object of her anger was that wretched being huddled in a corner. For if it had not been for him she would never have been in this situation. But for his uncontrolled temper, preceded by his lust for a girl less than half his age, neither of them would have been in this black-painted vehicle on their way to some place of incarceration and who could tell what forms of maltreatment.

It seemed a long journey. Perhaps imagination of what might be at the end made it appear longer than it was. It was possible to tell when they turned corners and when the horses struggled up hills, and now and then she heard the crack of the driver's whip.

The two plain clothes officers conversed in low tones, but Isabella could not hear what they were saying. They might have been discussing domestic matters that had nothing whatever to do with the job in hand. Such men, she supposed, must have private lives, but she found it hard to imagine them with wives and children.

At last they turned a sharp corner and rattled over more cobblestones and came to a halt. One of the policemen opened the door and got out. The one in plain clothes who seemed to be the highest ranking officer of the four ordered the two prisoners to follow him.

Isabella went first and discovered that they were in a large courtyard with high walls on three sides, in one of which was an iron gate giving access to a narrow lane outside. On the fourth side of the courtyard was a tall, bleak building, which made Isabella's heart sink by the mere sight of it.

All the windows in this building appeared to have bars

in them, and a door in the middle of the wall was studded with the heads of iron bolts. The entire outer side of this structure exhibited such a gloomy and forbidding aspect that it seemed to be saying: 'Abandon hope all ye who enter here'.

The interior, when they came to it, did nothing to dispel this impression. There was a damp, fusty odour about it, which might have come from the walls or the floor, or possibly the human beings who inhabited it. Some of these could be heard shouting or even screaming, though they could not be seen as one entered.

What could be seen was a long desk or counter, behind which was a fat uniformed policeman who appeared to be of higher rank than those who had accompanied the plain clothes officers. This man had a bushy moustache and mutton-chop whiskers. His nose was large and bulbous and the face was dotted here and there with warts, as though someone had started decorating it but had lost heart and left the job unfinished. He had a cold and kept wiping his nose on his sleeve.

There was a thick ledger on the desk in front of him, and it was in this that he wrote down the names and other particulars of the two prisoners. Maurat went first, and when asked the address of his residence he gave that of Isabella's apartment, which was a lie, and she felt an urge to contradict it. But she could not have told them where he had been living until the last few days because she did not know, and he was hardly likely to reveal it himself, since that was where the murder had taken place.

When it was her turn and she came to give her name as Isabella Jane Foster the man looked puzzled and she felt compelled to explain that she was English.

'Ah!' he said. And she wondered whether this would count against her.

When these preliminaries had been completed she and Maurat were separated and she was led away to find herself in a kind of iron-barred cage in which there were already some eight or nine creatures of a kind with which she had never previously rubbed shoulders. Some of them might have been young, but they all looked like hags; Macbeth's weird sisters multiplied by three. Their clothes were dirty rags and they were dirty themselves; their hair matted and greasy.

As soon as she entered they crowded round her, as though she were a creature from another world suddenly thrust into their company. Hands like claws with filthy broken nails stretched out to tug at the fabric of her dress which contrasted so sharply with the clothes which they were wearing.

'What you in for, dearie?' one of them asked.

She made no answer, but merely looked at them askance and tried to draw away from them. They cackled with laughter at this.

'Don't you like the company?' another asked. 'Not good enough for you? Well, you shouldn't have done what you did, then they wouldn't have pulled you in. Been a bad girl, have you? Oh, dear!'

The stench of their bodies and their rags nauseated her. She felt as if she was going to faint and she had to fight against it. Fortunately, after a while they seemed to lose interest in her and she withdrew to a corner where she waited with resignation for the next development.

It came before long. A saturnine officer unlocked the door of the cage and called her name. She answered immediately, thankful to be moved from that present company.

He relocked the door after she had joined him and conducted her down a corridor, round a corner and up a flight of stairs to a room with bare walls and one high window to let in the light. The furniture was spartan, consisting mainly of a deal table and two upright chairs.

There she was interrogated; she seated on one of the chairs and the interrogator, an officer in plain clothes, sitting on the other chair and facing her across the table. Meanwhile, the man who had escorted her to the room stood by the door looking bored by the whole proceeding.

The interrogator was a plump, middle-aged man with a bald head and a rather beaklike nose from which hairs protruded like little pieces of thin wire. There was something almost avuncular about him and he sighed now and then, as though he regretted the necessity of questioning such an attractive young woman on so distasteful a subject. But it had to be done.

'My name,' he said, 'is Vaudrin. Inspector Vaudrin.'

There was a pad of blotting-paper on the table in front of him, together with a notebook and an inkstand with a selection of pens in a rack. Now and then as he asked questions he dipped a pen in the ink and wrote somewhat laboriously in the notebook, apparently making a record of her replies.

'Why did you harbour a murderer in your apartment?'

'A murderer?'

'You did not know Monsieur Maurat had stabbed a young girl to death?'

'No.'

'But there was blood on his hands and his clothing, was there not?'

'Yes.'

'So how did you suppose it came there?'

'I didn't know.'

'You didn't ask him?'

'No.'

'Come, come,' Vaudrin said, giving a sadly admonishing shake of the head. 'That is really hard to believe. Now let us try to do better. I ask you again. How did he explain the blood?'

She hesitated, then said: 'I think he said he had cut himself accidentally.'

'But there were no cuts on him when he was arrested. They would have had to heal remarkably quickly, don't you think?'

She was silent.

'Now,' Vaudrin said, 'I am going to suggest that he really told you the truth concerning the origin of that blood. It was not his but someone else's, was it not?'

Still she was silent. What could she say?

'There is something that puzzles me,' Inspector Vaudrin said. 'Why in this extremity did he run to you for refuge?'

'I don't know.'

'Oh, I think you do. He knew you, didn't he?'

It would have been futile to deny it.

'Yes, he did.'

'How was that?'

'He used to live with me.'

'You were lovers?'

'I suppose you might say that.'

'But he left you?'

'Yes.'

'For a young girl?'

'I don't know.'

'Come, come! No more lies, please. You did know, and it must have irked you. Yet when he came running to you with blood on his hands you took him in and shielded him. That was really most generous of you. Some people, I might say most people, would have slammed the door in his face. But not you. You welcomed him in with open arms.'

She was stung to rebuttal. 'I did not. I did not. I wanted him to leave, but he would not. What was I to do?'

'You could have come to us.'

She was silent again.

'Did that not occur to you?'

It had, more than once. But she had never been able to bring herself to do it. She saw now how she had brought trouble on herself by not taking such action. And in the end she had not saved Maurat by not betraying him. So what in the end had either of them gained by her self-sacrifice?

The interrogation went on for some time longer, and Vaudrin did some more scratching with his pen. She could not tell whether he was satisfied or not, but in the end he let her go.

The officer who had been standing all this time took her in charge and they left the room. She was afraid he was going to take her back to the cage with the harridans, but he did not. Instead, he conducted her to a cell and locked her in.

The only thing that could have been said in its favour was that it was not the other place and there was no one to harass her. It was small and there was a hard bed with one grey blanket. The sanitary arrangements were primitive and there was a tiny barred window so high up that it was impossible to see out of it.

The cell was chilly and she shivered.

It was to be her home for the next six days.

31

FREEDOM

There was no more interrogation. She might have imagined that she had been shut away and forgotten if meals had not been brought to her regularly. She tried to get information from the officer who brought the food, but he would tell her nothing. He might as well have been a mute.

She wondered what the penalty might be for giving aid to a murderer. A long prison sentence? She tried to imagine what even one year shut up in a cell like this would do to one. It would be mental as well as physical torture. It would drive her out of her mind.

But it did not come to that. After six days they gave her back the key to her apartment and let her go.

There was no explanation. It just seemed that they no longer wanted her. Perhaps they needed the cell for someone else. She was not going to question the decision; she was only too happy to be released.

An officer conducted her to the gateway by which the

black van had entered, and when she had passed through the gate clanged shut behind her. It was a cold day and it was raining and she had neither coat nor hat. Moreover, she was ignorant of the way home. It took her more than two hours. She might have engaged a cab if she had had any money, but she had none. She had to make the journey on her own two feet, and by the time she reached home her shoes were in a sorry state and she was drenched to the skin. Her hand was shaking as she put the key in the lock and she could hardly turn it; but she got the door open and went inside.

Indoors it was scarcely warmer than it had been outside. The fire in the sitting-room had long since burned out and the cinders in the grate had an unwelcoming appearance. She was shivering uncontrollably, and before attempting to rekindle it she went to the bedroom, stripped to the skin and dried herself with a rough towel before finding some dry clothes to put on. Her hair was still damp and bedraggled but she would deal with that later. The next task was to get the fire going again.

Fortunately there was a supply of kindling and newspaper and it did not take long to have these blazing away and igniting the coal. She sank into the armchair and watched the flames, savouring the blessed feeling of being free again.

But still she could not understand why they had released her.

*

Some possible explanation came to her in the form of a newspaper which she bought the next day. It was an item of news which closely concerned her. There was a heading: 'MURDERER CONFESSES', and below it was a report that Jacques Maurat had confessed to the killing of Josephine Gautier with a kitchen knife.

So that was her name. It was odd that until that moment she had not known who the girl was that she had glimpsed only once in the street.

She read the report, but all she really needed to know was in the headline. He had confessed and it must have been decided that she had been punished enough.

She wondered what kind of pressure had been brought to bear on Maurat to persuade him to confess. Who could tell what went on in that forbidding building which she wanted never to enter again.

He would be executed of course. It would be a public exhibition and crowds would gather. But she would not be there. Nothing in the world would induce her to witness those last moments of Jacques Maurat's life.

Yet, when it came to the point, she went.

32

NOTORIETY

She would always remember that picture of him walking towards the guillotine with the priest reading from his book and walking backwards in front of him, as if to hide from his sight that lethal machine. At times he seemed to stumble, as though his legs had lost their strength, and she felt that she could detect the terror in his eyes even at such a distance.

She knew he was not a brave man. Those last days with him in the apartment had been evidence of that. So did they give the condemned man something to steady his nerves? A last drink of brandy, perhaps? Come what might, it had to be a dreadful ordeal, knowing that these were the last few steps of one's life before that lethal blade severed head from body.

In the end she did not see the final act of the drama. Even as the shining steel began to descend she lost consciousness. Did the executioner lift the head by its hair and exhibit it to the crowd, or was that simply a fable? She would never know.

She was not sure how long it was before she regained consciousness. It must have been quite a while, for the crowd had largely dispersed when she came to, and the guillotine was being dismantled. A woman was bending over her and fanning her with a glove. She was a stout, middle-aged person with a rosy face, and there was a man standing behind her who could have been her husband.

'Ah!' the woman said, 'She's waking up, poor soul.'

She was obviously speaking to the man, but then she addressed Isabella: 'We were beginning to be quite concerned about you, dear. You've been out so long. Been all too much for you, has it? The excitement.'

Isabella sat up, feeling sick. She struggled to her feet, the woman and the man helping her. There was mud on her coat, for the ground was dirty. She gazed about her.

'It is over?'

'Oh, yes,' the woman said. 'All over and done with. They've taken the body away. And the head too, of course. Don't know where they bury them. Do you, Jean?'

The man shook his head. 'In quicklime, so I've heard.'

Isabella shuddered at the thought of Jacques' body burning in quicklime.

The woman noticed. 'You're feeling cold. Better go home. Is it far? If it is, perhaps we could get a cab.'

'Oh, no. I can walk. It's not very far.'

'Well, if you say so. But you look a bit groggy to me. Are you sure you can make it?'

'Yes, quite sure. Thank you for helping me. I'm very grateful. I'll be on my way now.'

She wanted to be rid of them, to be alone. She started walking and the man and woman watched her for a while as if fearing she might fall. But when she did not they turned and walked off in the opposite direction.

It was a relief when she reached the apartment. She lit a fire and drank some wine and sat watching the coals burn. She wondered whether she would ever forget that last picture of Jacques walking towards the dread machine with its shining deadly blade. In wars men died in their thousands in all manner of horrible ways, but of course she had never been close to a war and the multitude of deaths she had not seen affected her far less than this solitary one to which she had been so close and so intimately involved. It would be in her dreams for a long time to come, even though she had not seen the head fall into the basket when the fatal cut was made she could certainly imagine it. And imagination was enough.

One result of the murder case, and it was a result she would gladly have gone without, was that she had become notorious in the neighbourhood in which she lived.

When she went out people stared at her as if she were

some kind of fairground monstrosity. She knew she was being talked about, though no one ever spoke to her, except a shop assistant here and there who could not avoid it.

But this phase was short-lived. Very soon the interest died down and she became as ignored as she had been before the murder. Again her existence was one of unrelieved boredom, a succession of days, weeks and months with scarcely anything to distinguish one from another.

She came to believe that it would go on like this indefinitely, and she became resigned to it. She was still far from old, but it was as if there was nothing left in life that was of any interest to her. Still, she supposed she was fortunate in having a comfortable home and a steady income. There were hundreds of poor wretches in Paris who were homeless and starving. She came across some of them now and then begging in the streets, and she gave them a coin or two to ease her conscience.

It did not occur to her then that she might ever become one of them.

The blow fell when one of those little slips of paper which she would take to the bank and exchange for cash failed to arrive on the date when it was due. She was not worried at first. It had been delayed, that was all. It would arrive later.

But it did not. Two weeks passed and still it had not come. She decided to make inquiries at the bank where she regularly cashed the cheques. She took with her the document that Maurat had handed to her to keep when the original deal had been made.

At the bank she showed this to one of the tellers whom she was familiar with and acquainted him with the situation.

'There should have been the regular payment two weeks ago, but it has not come.'

The teller, a middle-aged avuncular kind of man, looked at the document and shook his head sadly. It really seemed to grieve him to have to tell her the dismal truth.

'I fear, Madame, that there will be no more payments. The company has gone into liquidation. It was a gold-mining concern in Mexico, the kind of enterprise it is always risky to invest in. It appears the gold petered out and—' He gave a most expressive shrug of the shoulders which said all there was to say.

She was stunned. This could only mean that she was ruined. She stumbled out of the bank scarcely aware of where she was going. Somehow she reached home, went inside and collapsed in a chair.

It was hardly believable that it could all be gone; that now there would be no more money coming to her. She had never been in such a situation before, and it frightened her.

She blamed Maurat of course. He should have known it was a risky investment. He was supposed to be a financial expert, wasn't he? That was how he made a living, advising people on money matters. But perhaps it was because he was not very good at it that he had had so few clients and so much spare time.

She had been a fool to trust him. She saw that now, when it was too late. But he had been so persuasive and she so inexperienced in financial matters. Well, he was gone now, and she could not go to him for advice on how to climb out of the pit into which he had plunged her. She had to rely on her efforts to do so. And she could see no way.

33

THE SEINE

She sold the ring first. It was the one piece of jewellery she had retained when the rest had gone. She tried to haggle as Maurat had done, but she was no good at it and the jeweller knew that she would not hold out. He came back to the price he had originally offered her and she had to accept it.

The ring money kept her going for a while, but not for long. She sold the books next; but it was remarkable how much less you received for a book that had been read no more than once than you had paid for it when new. Moreover, many of her books had been secondhand when she bought them and were worth very little now.

She sold cutlery and bed-linen and china for next to nothing. She could not sell the furniture because the apartment had been taken furnished. She moved into cheaper accommodation in a less pleasant part of the city where she had never been before. She rubbed shoulders with the poor and was now one of them. She sold her clothes until she had only what she stood up in, and eventually she was evicted from the wretched lodging she was now living in because she had failed to pay the rent.

She was now on the streets, destitute and hungry, lacking even the skill to beg. She thought of the home in England that she had left so many years ago; and she knew that even that refuge was out of her reach, since she had no means to pay the expenses of travelling there.

It was as if by a kind of homing instinct that she found herself by the river. It was midnight, a thin rain falling, cold. There was a bridge. There were so many bridges across the Seine that you could hardly avoid finding one. She stepped on to the bridge and started walking. The bridge was only dimly lighted and the rain was falling more heavily now. If there were any other people about she failed to see them. She came to the middle and leaned on the parapet, gazing down at the dark water rushing past below her. Into her mind came the thought of Juliette LeBlanc and the failed artist from the apartment she had first shared with the girl. They had taken this way out and she would follow them, since life had become unbearable.

She climbed on to the parapet with the aid of a stanchion that supported one of the lamps. She stood there and looked down and heard someone shouting. It was a man's voice and there was a patter of feet, and then there was a hand clutching at her dress.

But it was too late; she had already released her grip on the stanchion and the clutching fingers could not hold her. Her dress billowed out as she fell; and then she was in the frigid water and being carried away by the current.

34

THE MORGUE

There were three naked bodies lying on the marble slab behind the plate-glass screen. Two were men, the third a woman. They were the latest harvest from the Seine, and they would lie there in the Morgue waiting for someone to walk in and claim them. If no one did so in the next day or two, they would be classified as unknown and would be taken away for burial in unhallowed ground on the outskirts of the city. No headstone would be erected to mark such a grave and the occupant would soon be forgotten.

A man came into the Morgue, nodded to the keeper and walked to the plate-glass screen. He was smartly dressed and might have been well past middle age. He hardly looked at the male bodies but he did look long and keenly at that of the woman, in whose features there was still some evidence that she had once been beautiful.

After a time he shook his head and muttered: 'No, it cannot be. And yet—'

He stayed there a while longer, then shook his head again and walked away.

The keeper of the Morgue watched him go. The woman would remain unknown.

35
A PITY

'It's a pity,' George said, 'that Aunt Maud couldn't tell us more about Bella. I wouldn't be surprised if she was really the most interesting one of the lot. A girl as pretty as that.'

Joyce laughed. 'Why, George, I do believe you've quite fallen in love with her.'

'Too late for that, isn't it? But I bet somebody did years ago. Maybe that's how it all started.'

'How what started?'

'Whatever it was that nobody mentioned in front of the children.'

'Maybe she ran away with a band of raggle-taggle gypsies-oh.'

'More likely a man.'

'And never came back?'

'Maybe. That's a thing about this family tree business. You may find out who your ancestors were and possibly how they got their living, but you really know nothing about their private lives. Like what time they got up in the morning, what they had for breakfast and what they talked about while they were eating it. Most of all, what did they do for amusement with no radio, no telly and all that. No telephones even to get in touch with one another.'

'And no washing-machines and no central heating. Must have been a tough life.'

'Possibly. But they wouldn't have been aware of it because it was all they'd ever been used to.'

'Now you're getting philosophical, George.'

'Maybe I am. But I'm thinking about this Bella.'

'Again?'

'Yes, again. Because we know absolutely nothing about her, except that when Aunt Maud was young nobody talked about her. So we just have this picture of her and nothing else. There's no record of her death, so we don't even know where she died. And now I suppose we shall never know that or anything more. It's so frustrating.'

'Well, that's the way it goes.'

'That's so. But it really is a pity.'

EPILOGUE

In World War Two a German shell landed on a piece of open ground on the outskirts of Paris. It left a deep crater and some mounds of loose earth in which were mingled fragments of human bones.

These fragments were all that was left of a woman who had once been a dancer at the Moulin Rouge. She had been known then by an adoring clientèle as L'Anglaise, but her real name was Isabella Foster and she was the daughter of an ironmonger in a small Norfolk village not many miles from the ancient city of Norwich.